"I'll never forget what it was like."

Years later, the hurt of his empty homecoming was reflected in Brad's eyes. "We got off the plane and there were hundreds of people waiting — families, loved ones — hugging and kissing, crying and laughing. I had some buddies waiting for me, but it wasn't the same as if somebody who loved me and cared about me had been praying for my safe return." He paused. "I shouldn't have expected...anyone."

"Brad," Sara said steadily, "I prayed for you. I wrote you a letter every day."

Agonized, he muttered, "I never received them."

"I loved you," Sara whispered. "As I loved Peter." She had loved him in a different way but she couldn't tell him that. "You *were* loved by someone."

Peter's Sister

Jeanne Allen

Harlequin Books

TORONTO • NEW YORK • LONDON
AMSTERDAM • PARIS • SYDNEY • HAMBURG
STOCKHOLM • ATHENS • TOKYO • MILAN

Original hardcover edition published in 1984
by Mills & Boon Limited

ISBN 0-373-02665-X

Harlequin Romance first edition January 1985

Printed in U.S.A.

CHAPTER ONE

SARA wanted desperately to wake up. The nightmare was beginning, but she was helpless to stop it. Even now she was two people; the one to whom the nightmare was happening, and the one who was watching. Peter and she were walking arm in arm. Peter's head was thrown back, his teeth gleamed in the sunlight, and she could hear his booming laughter. Something she'd said had amused him—she never knew what. Then he gestured, and her eyes followed his pointing finger. A man was approaching. The self that was watching tried to stop what was happening, but her other self hurried towards the man. He was young, and good-looking in a rakish sort of way. A lock of brown wavy hair dipped low over his right eyebrow, and the corners of his eyelids crinkled with laughter lines. Brown eyes gazed warmly at her, and he smiled as he held out his hand to her. Then his lips moved, and she strained to hear him speak—but she never heard the words. At that point, the smile disappeared, the eyes grew cold, a look of horror appeared, and then the face cracked and cracked until it finally broke into little pieces that fell into a pile at her feet. Terrified, she turned to Peter, only to find that he, too, had disappeared. The screaming woke her up.

As usual, Sara lay sweating, but chilled, in her bed waiting for the last vestiges of the nightmare to fade away. It wasn't until she'd had the dream several times that she had discovered that the screaming had come from her. It surprised her that no one else heard the piercing screams. Later the fact struck her that the screaming was only part of the dream.

She knew why she had the nightmare. She knew what it meant. She just didn't know how to prevent it. The nightmare had not occurred in a long time, and Sara had hoped the terrible dream had disappeared for ever. She must have dreamt it now, because tomorrow she was going to the Valley.

Sara Blanchard squinted fiercely into the blinding glare of the slowly setting sun. It was growing late, but she dared not press down harder on the accelerator; rushing heedlessly around the curves on these narrow Colorado mountain roads would be foolish. Soon the sun would set behind the tall peaks, and then she could make up a little lost time. Her intention had been to reach the Valley in mid-afternoon, but she had loitered in Denver, dreading her arrival at the old summer home. Now she would have to hurry or attempt the rocky road at night. The sun set early in the mountains, and when it did, darkness was total, especially on the tree-lined track that led to Blanchard Valley.

Blanchard Valley. Would it be peopled with the ghosts of Peter and her mother, and the memories of happier, bygone days? A sob rose in Sara's throat, and she hastily gulped it back. Ten long years had passed since she had visited the Valley. Ten years marked by pain, loneliness and death.

After her mother and Peter had died, Sara had felt that the only way that she could manage to go on with living was to replace her old memories with new ones. She had left Colorado and gone away to school. Her father had wanted her to try for a job in Denver, where he was a municipal judge, but she had refused. There were occasional flying trips back to see her father and her younger sister, Christy, but the visits were intentionally jam-packed with friends and activities. Anything to prevent remembering.

Her father seemed to understand and even to encourage Sara's attempts to completely erase the past. He, too, had made changes. A professional decorator had come in and totally redone the house, removing all traces of Mrs Blanchard and Peter. Sara could stay at the house and never worry that she might go through a door and be confronted with her mother's favourite chair, or turn a corner and see Peter's old football trophies. The home had become a house, a place she visited.

When Sara and her father met, they talked only of the present. It was as if an unspoken agreement prevented them from discussing the past. Sara's sister had been a child at the time of the double tragedy, and she had joined in the conspiracy of silence, although mostly through lack of memories, Sara felt. Lately Sara had come to wonder whether they had been wrong to try and wipe out old, good memories. Maybe remembering the good times would have eased the way for them both to have fully grieved, and then, the grieving over, to get on with their lives.

As she drove, she recalled her last visit to Blanchard Valley. Peter had been in Vietnam then, so there had been just the four of them, Sara, Christy, the Judge and Mrs Blanchard. They had gone to the Valley to stay for two weeks, but had returned to Denver in less than one. No one had enjoyed the stay. Everyone had moped about missing Peter, until finally Sara's mother had packed them up and back to Denver where, at least, there were friends and diversions. Unspoken was the thought that they wouldn't go back until Peter returned. Only Peter had not returned, and the Blanchards had not gone again to Blanchard Valley.

Last summer the Judge had tentatively suggested that they vacation together at the Valley, but Christy was involved with a summer job, and Sara had quickly made plans for a trip to Hawaii. When Sara had gone to Denver this last Christmas, she had mentioned that perhaps they should sell the Valley, but the Judge had quietly refused and changed the subject.

Therefore it shouldn't have been totally unexpected when the Judge had written and said he planned to spend the summer at the Valley. He had retired from the judicial bench in January and was finding himself at a loose end.

Sara had read the letter through in uneasy anticipation, but her father only discussed his fishing plans. Dread returned with his next letter, which mentioned that Christy had decided to forgo her usual summer job and stay with him at the Valley. The Judge wrote that Christy didn't seem to think that, in the circumstances, their housekeeper was capable of looking after him at the Valley, which was ridiculous, but there was no changing Christy's mind.

'What circumstances?' Sara had wondered in bewilderment. A call home had answered her question. It seemed that the Judge had paid his doctor a visit, and there was talk of a heart condition.

'Nothing serious,' her father assured her. 'Nothing for you to worry about.' She hadn't believed him, and the fear that her father might die haunted her. So when he had asked, much too casually, about her summer plans and said that it was too bad that she wouldn't have a chance to join him and Christy for the summer, she had heard herself informing him that she, too, was going to the Valley.

As her vacation approached, she found herself, one moment, bitterly resenting her father's state of health forcing her to return to Colorado, even though she knew that was unfair. The next moment, a tiny hidden burst of joy would erupt at the thought of seeing the magical valley again. The ambivalent feelings had warred within her, making her edgy and uncertain, until the emotional stress had stretched her nerves thin to the breaking point. They had finally snapped last night when Roger, who rarely failed to sense her every mood, had proposed to her once gain. She had lashed out at him, making him the target for her frustrations. Dear, kind, steady Roger who thought if he were patient enough he could wear down Sara's resistance. Roger Matthews had wealth, breeding, intelligence and compassion, and was a witty and considerate companion. She was a fool to keep turning down his frequent marriage proposals.

Sara sighed. Roger had suggested that he fly out to the Valley and join her for a few days. They had had their first bitter argument when she had abruptly refused, and she had been cruel enough to say that they didn't want an outsider at Blanchard Valley. He had accused her of being obsessed with her brother's death, and he had called her a coward who was afraid to love. He was right, of course. Love hurt. Sara refused to be hurt again, but it wasn't loving Peter that had damaged her. It was loving a man Roger had never heard of, a man named Brad Rawlins. Even after all these years, the merest thought of Brad, and instantly his face flashed across her mind—the wavy hair, the laughing eyes, the magic smile.

No! Her clenched fist hit the steering wheel. It was time to break the fetters of the past. When she reached the house she would call Roger and tell him to come out for a few days. If Christy and the Judge approved— well, maybe the next time Roger proposed marriage, he would receive a different answer. Hard work and determination had propelled Sara to her present position, but lately a bothersome imp of dissatisfaction had nagged at her. Marrying Roger might instil a sense of direction in her life. Making the decision comforted her, and she thought maybe the visit wouldn't be so difficult after all. Roger wouldn't allow old remembrances to haunt her, and together they could start building towards new memories.

Sara dragged her thoughts back to her surroundings. Somewhere soon should be the entrance to the Valley. Just in time she noticed the break in the trees and sharply swung the wheel. Slowly and cautiously, she negotiated her way up the rock-strewn road, wincing as low-hanging branches scraped the sides of the car and gasping as she jerked the wheel to avoid large boulders only to land in deep holes. The fact that daylight had all but faded away made the trip up the mountain seem eerie, with the only sounds those of the roar of the laboured car engine and the slapping of the branches against the car. After what seemed an eternity, the car topped a crest, and there spread out before her was Blanchard Valley. Far down the Valley she could see the twinkling lights in the old ranch house.

The road felt smoother here, and she carefully speeded up, pulling up to the large frame house with a flourish and a scattering of gravel. A sense of homecoming radiated from the old white summer home. Suddenly she felt her father was right in gathering the remnants of the family back here. Tears threatened as she realised how much she had missed this lovely place. In quickening anticipation, she beeped the car horn and jumped out of the car yelling, 'Anybody home?'

'Sara!' the loud shriek preceded her sister as Christy came flying out of the screen door, the door crashing unheeded back against the outside wall. 'Why are you so late? We've been worried! I thought you'd never get here! Isn't it great that you could get one whole glorious month off this summer? Daddy and I are both thrilled, and wait till you see who's here . . .'

'Welcome home, Sara,' Judge Blanchard's calm voice broke into Christy's bubbling stream of words.

Sara disengaged herself from her sister's rough squeezes and rushed up the steps to embrace her father. 'Daddy, you look marvellous!' she said as she put her hands on his shoulders and stepped back to survey his handsome tanned face, anxiously searching for any sign of his heart condition. 'Retirement must agree with you,' she added deliberately in a light tone as she scanned his face to see if he flinched at the word retirement.

He only hugged her to him again, then flung an arm about her shoulders and guided her into the house. 'We can get the luggage later. You must be exhausted after driving all day. Besides, there's someone I want you to meet.'

Sara frowned and pulled back. 'I thought it would be just family this summer, Daddy.'

'That was my intention, but—well, this is someone very special.' He urged her on into the house.

Knowing the first step across the threshold would be the hardest, Sara reluctantly entered the large foyer, and was immediately engulfed by warm and welcome feelings of nostalgia. Sighing in contentment, she let her gaze roam over the worn Turkish carpet, the wide steep stairs leading to the second floor, and the ancient grandmother clock on the wall ticking its way towards eight o'clock. She looked around at her father's anxious face and took a deep breath. 'It's good to be here,' she said simply.

Her father smiled, and she saw how tense he had been.

'I think it will be okay, Sara,' he said as he held her close again. Then clasping her arm lightly, he pulled her to the nearest doorway, Christy following them with an eager look on her face.

Conflicting emotions raged within Sara as she stepped through the doorway into the living room. Generations of Blanchards had imprinted a personality on the room that would have been envied by any interior decorator striving for the 'country manor' look. The only illumination in the darkened room was provided by the flames from the mammoth fireplace.

A grey-haired man arose from the Victorian settee near the fire. This stranger's intrusion into her first night back at the Valley annoyed Sara. She cocked a questioning eyebrow at her father, then turned to greet the elderly gentleman.

As the man came nearer and the light from the hall struck his face, she noticed how his eyes crinkled at the corners, and his greying hair waved. He slowly smiled and opened his mouth to speak, and cracks spread down one side of his face.

Sara screamed. The horror of it was an almost physical blow to her stomach. She clenched her fist to her mouth to stop herself from screaming as her nightmare came to life. The light from the hall began to dance wickedly past her eyes, then the fireplace and the chairs joined and circled about her. She caught glimpses of Christy and her father staring in open-mouthed amazement. Again the man started to speak, and mercifully, the room went black.

Sara heard voices, but she stubbornly resisted opening her eyes. Waves of nausea still rolled over her, and she was afraid if she opened her eyes she would see *him*, and the furniture would start its weird dancing again. There was an irritating buzz, and she was aware that her dad was speaking.

'Sara—Sara! Are you okay?'

'Maybe some water,' a deep voice suggested.

'I'll get it.'

Sara heard Christy run clomping from the room. Wooden sandals obviously were in this summer, she thought absurdly, her mind determined to evade the reality of his presence.

'I don't understand it. I don't think Sara has ever fainted before.'

Was that anxious, fretful voice her father's? She must open her eyes and reassure him. Worry would be bad for his heart.

'I told Sara driving all the way in one day was too much,' her father continued in a worried voice.

'It was a mistake not to have warned her that I was here.'

That deep voice again. Strange how you could know about the life, the thoughts, the face of a person and never have heard his voice. Sara had many times tried to imagine the sound, high-pitched or low, maybe an accent, but had always to give up in futility. And now, after all these years, to hear it from this grey-haired man who wore scars and lines not natural for a man of his age. James Bradley Rawlins. How different he looked from his photograph taken ten years ago. Different, and yet the same.

The voices around Sara continued to quietly mutter. She opened her eyes a slit and curiously gazed at the face of the man she had loved with such total joy and abandon. 'James Bradley Rawlins.' She must have said his name out loud.

He leaned down to her. 'I apologise, Sara. We should have let you know I'd be here.' He helped her to a sitting position and studied her, his face impassive.

'Why are you here?' Could that hoarse voice be coming from her?

'I see you recognise me,' he evaded. 'I thought you might not, as I've changed so much since that picture was taken.'

The picture that Brad meant seared across Sara's brain, and for a second she saw the young smiling man, unscarred by life. Unable to stop herself, she reached out and traced the scars down the side of his face, the scars that she had thought were cracks when she had first seen them. Her fingers seemed to burn with the contact, and she felt Brad flinch at her touch. 'Did they do that to you?' she asked in a trembling voice.

'Shrapnel,' he answered tersely. He tried for a lighter touch. 'I've been told it gives me a debonair look.'

Her eyes flew to his hair—abundant, wavy and streaked with grey. What must a man suffer to cause his hair to become grey at such an early age? She shuddered at the horrors evoked by the thought.

He misunderstood. 'It does look rather shocking. I'll grow into it as the years pass. When I'm eighty and bald, I'm sure I'll wish I still had it, no matter the colour!'

'How can you joke about it? It's horrible, disgusting . . .' her tight voice faded away.

In a voice devoid of emotion, Brad answered, 'I've had years to get used to it. I forget how it might offend someone seeing me for the first time.'

Sara gasped. 'I . . . I didn't . . . I didn't mean . . .' she floundered, distressed at the pain she saw in his eyes.

'Don't worry about it. I'm used to some women shuddering when they see me.'

'I didn't shudder. Well, maybe I did, but . . .' Sara tried weakly to explain her shock.

Brad just shrugged as if her opinion didn't matter to him, and then he was shouldered aside as Christy returned with a glass of water.

Grasping the glass with a shaky hand, Sara sipped at the cooling liquid, then smiled wanly into her father's apprehensive face peering around Brad and Christy. 'I'm okay, Dad. I must have pushed myself too hard today.' She tried to concentrate on her father, but her eyes were irresistibly drawn to Brad. She summoned every ounce of control she possessed to keep from reaching out and touching him again. His watching face seemed to her to mock her efforts, and an overwhelming urge to escape drove her from the couch. 'If you don't mind, Dad, I think I'll skip dinner and go right to bed.'

'I think you ought to eat something,' the Judge said uneasily.

'Daddy, I'll take Sara a tray up later,' Christy offered.

Sara moved cautiously, relieved to find that the room fixtures remained in place. 'Nice to finally meet you, Brad,' she smiled fixedly in his general direction and then crossed the large room in careful little steps.

There was a slight snort behind her, then she gasped as she was swept up off her feet.

'Nice to meet you at last, Sara,' Brad mimicked.

At his touch, feverish waves of unidentified longings tore through her body, startling her with their intensity. 'Put me down!' she ordered shakily.

'I'm just helping you up the stairs. The way those legs of yours are wobbling, you'll never make it.'

Indignation momentarily smothered her voice. 'I can too walk. Put me down!' She strained to free herself from the strong arms that imprisoned her.

'Sara, I think you're overwrought. Be a good girl and let Brad help you to your room. I certainly don't want to start off this summer with you falling down the stairs!'

Sara started to protest, but then she remembered the Judge's heart condition and noticed his face, now white and drawn. Clenching her lower lip between her teeth, she remained silent while Brad carried her out of the room. As he laboured up the steep staircase, his heart pounded through his heavy woollen shirt. She prayed that he wouldn't notice her own traitorous erratic heartbeat. Closing her eyes, she fought against an unnerving desire to melt into his arms.

'There, now was that so bad?' Brad set her on her feet.

Sara seethed as she realised that he was watching with callous amusement her struggle for self-control. 'Thank you,' she said coldly.

'You don't sound very grateful,' he observed. 'I carried you up a very steep flight of stairs. You may be a skinny little thing,' he smiled at her indignant denial, 'but you're no lightweight! I think I deserve a more tangible sign of appreciation, like a kiss.'

She understood at once that he wanted to punish her for what he thought was her revulsion when she had first seen his scars. Backing away, she shook her head.

'Not even a brotherly kiss?' he teased.

His taunting words loosened Sara's fingernail clutch at restraint, and to her dismay, terrible, shrieking words tumbled unchecked from her lips. 'My brother is dead! You are not my brother, and never will be. You, of all people, should know never to talk to me of my brother! Now get out of here!' she spat, unable to stop herself. 'I don't want you here. Why should you be here when Peter can't be?'

Brad's face seemed to wither and die before her eyes. Just like her nightmare. A cold desolate look settled over his features, chilling the very marrow of her bones. He turned to leave the room, and tentatively, she reached out her hand and touched his arm. 'I'm sorry, Brad. Please forgive me. I'm tired—I didn't mean what I said.'

Brad paused, but didn't look at Sara. 'I'll bring up your bags,' he said in an empty voice.

Sara's legs did give out then, and she sank gratefully

on to the nearby bed. Her head was swimming in confusion. What was Brad doing in Blanchard Valley? As she tried to sort out her chaotic thoughts, not the least of which dealt with her powerful reaction to Brad's touch, several minutes elapsed before she realised that someone was knocking on her bedroom door.

She made several attempts before she finally managed a hoarse, 'Come in.'

Christy manoeuvred her way past the bedroom door, her hands loaded down with a very full tray that threatened to dump its contents any minute. Greatly relieved that the visitor was not Brad, Sara quickly rescued the tray and set it on the wicker table in front of the window.

'Now tell me,' Christy ordered in a conspiratorial manner. 'I know who Brad is, and why he is here, but what I don't know is what he is to you. The look on your face when you saw him . . .' Her voice trailed off as she eyed Sara curiously.

'I don't know what you mean.' Sara busied herself buttering a slice of bread.

'Love, ecstasy, joy, call it what you want. Then, suddenly, total horror—you scream, and flop, over you go on the floor. Well, not exactly on the floor, because Brad caught you,' Christy conceded. 'How do you know him? He's never been to visit before.' She wrinkled up her pert little nose. 'At least, I don't remember him.'

Sara sighed. She'd have to tell Christy the whole story. If she didn't her sister was fully capable of repeating her questions to Brad. 'It was so long ago,' she mused half to herself. 'Peter . . .' her voice faltered.

'Peter? What does Peter have to do with it?'

'It all began because of Peter. Peter and the Vietnam war. You were so young at the time, only nine. I was sixteen. Peter was twenty-two, just out of college when he enlisted as an officer in the Air Force. He graduated from pilot training and was sent directly to Vietnam in a fighter, to a place called Da Nang.

'I guess I was what you'd call an impressionable teenager, but I adored Peter. He was so gay and handsome. All the girls chased after him during his last leave home, but usually I was the one he took places. I understand now that I was his safeguard against being involved. Then—well, I guess I thought I was pretty special. All my friends envied me.' Sara managed a wan smile. 'It's a wonder I didn't trip over my own feet, my smug nose was so high in the air!'

'But what does all this have to do with Brad?' Christy interrupted.

'I can tell you faster if you'll keep quiet.'

'All right, go ahead.'

'When Peter left, the whole family was despondent. Mother and Daddy tried so hard to comfort each other and remain cheerful. You were just confused. And as for me—well,' Sara said ruefully, 'I must have been a pain in the neck. Every time Mom asked me to do something I said I had to write to Peter. And I did. I wrote daily. Peter was not so faithful. Of course, he was busier than I was, but I guess my daily letters and begging for answers were making him feel awfully guilty.

'Brad was Peter's room-mate in their billeting quarters. Because he didn't have any living relatives, Brad didn't receive much mail, so Peter had the brilliant idea to get Brad and me to be pen-pals.' Sara paused as her thoughts returned to the past. She had welcomed the notion of writing to Brad, and their friendship had blossomed amid the horrors of war. At first she had continued to write to Peter, but encouraged by Brad's prompt answers, she had concentrated her efforts on his behalf while her letters to her brother had dwindled down to almost nothing. Soon she was telling all her thoughts to Brad, savouring all the incidentals of her daily life to tell him. All that occurred around her was immediately translated in her mind into an amusing tale to pass on to Brad. He wrote back his feelings about the conflict and expressed his loneliness at having no family, as he was an only child whose parents had been killed in a traffic accident while he was in college. She had spent hours buying clever notecards and clipping interesting articles to send to him. In the mail, pictures of a fresh young girl in a cheer-leading outfit passed pictures of a handsome young aviator leaning casually against a jet fighter. When Sara looked at that photograph, she had thought of old war movies where the heroes were strong and handsome and brave, and she knew that Brad was like that. She fell in love with his picture and the dark wavy hair which threatened to flop over into his eyes, the straight shiny teeth and the smile that winged its way direct to her heart.

'Well, were you?' Christy asked impatiently.

'Were we what?'

'Pen-pals! What are we talking about anyway?'

'Oh, I'm sorry. Yes, we were. Brad and I corresponded until he was shot down in combat. Peter wrote and told me that Brad was missing in action, and then, a few days later, Peter was also shot down.'

'It's so awful,' Christy's eyes misted. 'I knew that Brad had been a friend of Peter's and a P.O.W.'

Sara barely heard her, her mind caught up in the past. 'Brad was a P.O.W. like Peter . . . only Brad lived to make it home. Poor Peter!' Her voice caught in a sob. Wrenching pangs of guilt still tore through her when she recalled neglecting her brother to write to Brad. Brad, who had proved so unworthy.

'Do you suppose prison camp is why Brad's hair is so grey?' mused Christy. 'He can't be thirty-five years old yet, and even though that's old, it's not that old.'

'I suppose so. The rest of us can't imagine what they went through. I used to have nightmares about it.' Sara neglected to mention that her nightmares still continued. The dream probably symbolised her abandoning Peter and choosing Brad, only to lose them both.

Christy sighed and was quiet for a few minutes.

Sara was remembering those horrible days when they had first heard that Peter was missing in action, and the long, torturous months that followed. Waiting for news had been agony. Her mother had kept the family going, always maintaining that there was hope, until one morning she had opened the newspaper and read an article about the latest battle and casualties. The article was no better and no worse than stories of previous weeks, but her mother's spirit had broken, and she had gone to bed and died. The doctor had called it a heart attack.

'What happened then? Sara—I asked, what happened then?'

Christy's persistent questioning forced Sara back to the present. 'I'm sorry, Christy. What did you ask?'

'What happened when Brad came back?'

Sara noticed dispassionately that her hands were trembling, and she put down her spoon. 'Nothing,' she answered in a quiet voice. 'I never heard from Brad again. I knew he'd returned because I saw his name in the newspaper.' Her memories were still painful to Sara. When the P.O.W.s were finally released, she had been in the hospital recovering from an emergency appendectomy. Her father had withheld the newspapers for days, and then had gently told her that Peter had died in the prison camp. Even as she had grieved for her brother, she had pored over the published list of released P.O.W.s and had been exultant to find Brad's name among them. Guiltily, she had nursed her secret joy as all about her mourned Peter's death.

Christy was confused. 'But surely Brad called or tried to look you up?'

Sara managed a laugh. 'I'm sure when he returned he was much too busy to worry about a teenage pen-pal.' She still remembered the breathless anticipation that had faded to despair when Brad had failed to contact her. He didn't call. He didn't write. He didn't come. She had been sure that he would rush to her side—and his rejection had devastated her. Her heart burned with shame as she pictured the amusement he must have derived from the half-baked dribble she'd written him.

In his loneliness, he had used her, and when his need was gone, discarded her. Crying herself to sleep at night, she had been tormented with visions of him in the arms of an older woman.

Christy frowned. 'I'd think he'd at least have written you a note.'

'I'm sure after being a prisoner for almost two years, Brad had totally forgotten about me,' Sara shrugged.

'Why didn't you write to him?'

'How could I? I didn't know where to write.' Trying to contact Brad had turned out to be an insurmountable problem. Feeling unable to approach her bereft father for help, in desperation Sara had written Brad a letter and mailed it to the Pentagon. Months later it was returned, unopened, stamped 'Addressee not at this address'. Sara now looked out the window, away from Christy's inquisitive eyes. 'Anyway, you can see why it was such a shock to see Brad in person after all these years.'

'I suppose so,' Christy returned doubtfully.

She wanted to pursue the subject, and it seemed like for ever before Sara could persuade her to leave. When Christy finally gave up and departed, Sara dragged herself into the white-tiled bathroom. After filling the old claw-legged iron tub with hot water, she stepped out of her clothes and eased her body beneath the layer of soap bubbles. With a towel acting as a cushion behind her head, she leaned back to soothe away the aches of her tired body, and wearily closed her eyes. Brad's faces, then and now, whirled faster and faster about in her head until they collided and splintered apart, only to rejoin in yet another mad kaleidoscope. She shook her head in a futile effort to clear her mind of the dizzying tumult.

To have Brad turn up now was a shock. Why was he here? She berated herself for failing to ask more questions of Christy. Was Brad married? Where was his family? Why was he here in the Valley?

Anger rose in her throat at the knowledge that

regardless of his past cavalier treatment of her, she could still be betrayed into a physical response to his presence. Unbidden, the warning edged into her mind that such a reaction to Brad's touch was dangerous, and her stomach contracted in fear.

She must not panic. Surely those inexplicable feelings could be dismissed as mere chemistry. Once a person had a disease and recovered from it, they were no longer susceptible, just as she was immune now to Brad's handsome smile. His considerable charm, a charm which admittedly was not diminished one whit by his scars, could not affect her now. Roger was her talisman against the purely physical attractions of Brad, and she clung to the thought of Roger as an island of safety in a battering sea of treacherous emotions and undercurrents which threatened to sweep her heedlessly along. Roger's gentle countenance swam before her eyes and then was edged away by Brad's mocking face. She slapped the water with her flannel and spoke out loud: 'It's only chemistry.' She refused to allow herself to dwell on the fact that, with Roger, there was no such chemistry.

The next morning found Sara still trying to convince herself that Brad's presence in the Valley meant nothing to her. A restless night had ill prepared her for a second confrontation with him, and she dreaded going downstairs, although she knew she must face him sooner or later. Let it be later. Brad Rawlins was ancient history, she repeated over and over to herself. She had recovered from her childish infatuation, but the guilt and embarrassment lingered on. She didn't care one bit about Brad, but no one liked being an object of pity or ridicule, she told herself, stoking her anger as a protective cloak. Brad had probably known of her crush and even now was secretly laughing at her. But why was he here?

Playing for time, Sara slowly unpacked her suitcases which had been placed in her room the previous night while she was bathing. She carefully hung dresses and blouses in the tall armoire that served as a closet. The room had changed little over the years. The valuable old carved oak pieces had been brought to Colorado on a wagon train by early Blanchard relatives. Ruffled white dotted Swiss curtains at the window swinging in the morning breeze were new, but the log cabin patterned quilt in shades of blue had been painstakingly hand-stitched by her great-grandmother. Oval braided rag rugs of blues and reds were scattered like jewels on the glossy pegged wood floors. A sampler hanging over her bed looked charming in spite of, or because of, the glaring mistakes stitched into it by a long-forgotten aunt. On top of the armoire lolled two rag dolls, their stitched grins mocking her lack of courage.

Sighing, Sara searched through her wardrobe for suitable clothes. Already the July day gave indication of being scorching hot, so she pulled on white canvas shorts and a yellow gingham top. Quickly running a comb through her tousled hair and touching her lips with coral lipstick, girded herself to leave the room.

To her relief, only her father was in the dining room, reading a newspaper and munching a crisp piece of toast. He didn't notice her entering the room, and she quietly moved up behind him and bent to kiss the nape of his neck. 'Good morning, Daddy. Where is everyone? Don't tell me I'm so late they're all gone.' With every appearance of gaiety, she poured herself coffee from the pot on the sideboard and sat down at the round oak table. A silver-covered casserole was reflected in the shiny golden-hued wood, and she lifted the lid and sniffed appreciatively at the creamy scrambled eggs and ham prepared by Mrs Collins, the housekeeper.

'Good morning, Sara dear, are you feeling better this morning?' Her father eyed her with concern as he peered over his reading glasses.

'Tip-top on this glorious morning,' she assured him.

'Good, good. And to answer your question, it's not late, only half-past seven, as a matter of fact. Christy is, of course, still in bed and will be for hours. How that child can sleep her life away is beyond me! The morning is the best part of the day. You people who sleep in don't know what you're missing.'

Sara chuckled. 'Still an early riser trying to convert us old slugabeds, I see!' She smiled affectionately at her father, noticing how distinguished he appeared even in his well-worn khaki outdoor shirt. Over the years the military-looking brass buttons had been lost one by one, to be replaced by a motley assortment of blue, brown and white buttons. 'Really, Dad,' she admonished, 'don't you think you can afford a new shirt by now?'

'This one is just getting comfortable. It has at least ten more years of wear in it,' the Judge answered complacently. 'Besides, if you think my shirt looks worn, wait until you see the many-patched splendours of Christy's jeans. Sometimes I suspect she puts patches where no holes even exist. That child!' He shook his head in amused perplexity.

Sara spread her toast with peach jam. 'You'd better quit calling her "that child", or she'll be up in arms! She's almost twenty now, and will be a junior at the University.'

'I know, I know. But sometimes twenty seems so young to me.'

'You and Mom were twenty when you decided to get married,' Sara reminded him.

'That was different. We were an old twenty.' His eyes twinkled in acknowledgment of the absurdity of his rebuttal.

There was a companionable silence as the Judge returned to his paper, and Sara finished her breakfast. She was drinking her after-breakfast coffee before she had gathered enough courage to approach the subject she was most interested in. 'Where's Mr Rawlins, Dad? Has he eaten, or is he a late riser, too?'

'Oh no, Brad gets up with the chickens. He isn't here because he eats breakfast in the guest cabin where he's staying. So he won't bother us, he says, but personally, I think he was afraid Christy would pester him and this old man would bore him with reminiscences.'

'Pooh,' Sara scoffed. 'You know you couldn't bore anyone.'

The Judge smiled his appreciation before returning the conversation back to Brad. 'He's Colonel Rawlins now. He was promoted early, due to his wartime experiences, I would imagine.'

'But why is he here? I thought we were to be just family this summer. Why isn't Brad with his own family? Having him here will just ruin our summer!' Even as Sara noted how childish she sounded, she hoped that her father wouldn't notice that she had called Brad by his first name.

'To answer your last question first, Brad has no family living, and he's never married. As to the rest,' her father answered slowly, marshalling his thoughts, 'you remember how upset and in what turmoil everything was back then, what with your mother dying so suddenly, and then Peter . . . At first, I didn't want to know anything, and I just wanted to forget that entire part of our life. I was almost happy that your mother had died.' The Judge held up his hand at Sara's small moan. 'Now, Sara, you know what I mean. Your mother had already suffered so much worrying about Peter that she could never have withstood the final blow of his death.'

'What does that have to do with Brad being here?' asked Sara in bewilderment.

Judge Blanchard frowned at the interruption. 'A year ago I noticed an article in the newspaper about a former P.O.W. who was speaking to a ladies' group in Denver. The talk was open to the public, so I decided to go, and it turned out that Brad was the speaker.'

'You went to a ladies' meeting?' Sara was incredulous.

'The ladies just sponsored it. The talk was open to the public, and many men were present.'

'Why would you go to something like that?'

'It's hard to explain this to you, Sara, but for some time I'd been feeling uneasy in my mind about Peter, as if I'd let him down. I told myself I should have found out more about the circumstances of his death. I thought that this talk might clear up some questions, and although I didn't know Brad, I hoped that maybe an ex-P.O.W. could somehow help me. I'd finally realised that I needed to face up to the truth of Peter's death.'

'What did Brad talk about?'

'He touched lightly on his experiences, but mostly he talked about duty and honour.'

'Dull stuff,' Sara scoffed.

'Yes,' her father agreed, 'it sounds that way, but it wasn't. I can't really explain it, but Brad's words were truly inspirational, and I was extremely moved. I would like to think that Peter felt the same way about his sacrifices as did Brad.'

'Dad! Peter was the bravest, the most honourable, the . . . the . . .' Sara spluttered in her indignation.

Judge Blanchard held up his hand to silence the incoherent flow of words. 'Sara, do you want to hear this story or not?'

'I'm sorry.' She subsided back into her chair.

'I arranged for Brad and myself to meet, and with Brad I discovered that I could talk about Peter. All these years I've skirted around my loss, taken down Peter's pictures to spare the whole family, and nothing has helped to ease the ache. In fact,' her father added in a heavy voice, 'I did about everything wrong when we lost Peter and your mother. I should have aired my grief and encouraged you to do the same. Hiding from reality, as we both did, wasn't healthy for either of us. 'I've made many mistakes in my life, Sara, but this is the one that I regret the most.'

'Oh, Daddy,' Sara faltered as she herself had wondered these same thoughts lately. Vaguely she realised that her father was still speaking.

'Brad and I began a very satisfactory correspondence. I didn't mention all this to you, because—well, quite frankly, Sara, I was sure you'd disapprove.' He paused. 'I only recently discovered that you and Brad are acquainted. I knew that you'd been writing to a friend of Peter's in Vietnam, but I never paid any attention to the name, and only realised who you were writing to when Brad mentioned it the other day.'

'What did he say?' asked Sara, in spite of herself.

'It was just a passing reference, but it made me stop and think, Sara.' The Judge rose and came around the table to where she sat, and placed his hands on her shoulders. 'Apparently you and Brad were on friendly terms at one time, and even though you've grown apart, I'd like you to spend some time with Brad and get to know him again.'

'Why?' Sara asked tersely.

'I know how you miss Peter, Sara. You've been like me and put him out of your life. It's time to bring him back and let his memory live openly in your heart and thoughts. Please talk to Brad about Peter.'

'No, no—I can't!' Sara cried as she gazed at her father in consternation. Sara might kid herself that her old wounds had healed, but she wasn't fool enough to think that she would survive a month in Brad's constant company without somehow revealing what a fool she'd been in the past. Even now, she found that she wanted desperately to ask why Brad had never contacted her when he had returned. Bringing up the war and Peter was sure to open old wounds best left undisturbed.

The Judge looked disappointed. 'I won't push you, Sara. I had hoped that you were ready to deal with Peter's death, but apparently you aren't.' He paused, then continued quietly, 'Sara, Peter has been dead almost nine years. You must learn to face that fact.'

Her father's words of disapproval turned Sara to stone as he left the dining room. If only he understood! If only she could explain how it was to him. Brad had

shattered her life once. Because of him, she had
neglected her own brother, and later, guilt about that
neglect had plunged her to the depths of suffering.
Years of pain, of struggle had been endured as piece by
piece she had rebuilt her life trying to fill the deep void
left by the loss of both men.

She had resigned herself, even begun to look forward
to this vacation. Why, oh why, if the Judge had needed
to talk with an ex-P.O.W., did he have to choose Brad,
of all people? She could not allow Brad to disrupt her
life again. He had no power over her now and must
never know about the power he had held in the past,
the power he had cavalierly discarded. Even though she
no longer loved him, his humiliation of her was still a
painful thorn in her side.

CHAPTER TWO

AFTER breakfast Sara wandered disconsolately about
the house, until at length she ventured into the large
living room. Emotionally overwrought the previous
night, she had barely noticed her surroundings. The
room was light and airy, with whitewashed pine walls
and an abundance of large multi-paned windows.
Opposite the doorway where she was standing, two
French doors led to the veranda and a magnificent view
of Red Mountain. Centred on the long wall of the room
was the huge stone fireplace already set with fresh logs
in preparation for the evening's chill. A pair of
mismatched Victorian settees upholstered in a blue and
white fabric flanked the fireplace, anchored in place by
a wine-red Oriental rug. A Queen Anne fireside bench
was covered in faded blue needlepoint done by an
earlier Blanchard lady.

Charming as the room was, it seemed somehow
different to Sara, and she wrinkled her brow in
concentration. Suddenly her eyes stopped roaming the
room and were locked on the walls above and beside
the fireplace. The heads were missing. For as long as
she could remember, that particular wall had been
adorned with numerous mounted trophies: deer, elk,
moose, antelope, even trout and a large grizzly bear had
smirked down on the room's inhabitants. Now the wall
was covered with framed photographs. Sara moved
closer. Someone had hung a collection of her pictures
all over the wall. They were pictures that she had
snapped years ago, and all had the same theme—they
had been taken here in the Valley, taken in earlier,
happier years. Sara studied the collection of photographs, stopping in shock in front of a picture that she
remembered well. Of her brother Peter, the photo had

been taken the summer before he had left, and caught the essence of the fun-loving aspect of Peter's personality, as he had posed for the camera showing off with mock pride a four-inch trout. Oh, Peter, Sara cried silently, I miss you so! Tears streamed down her face as she slowly discovered other photos of her brother scattered throughout the display. Here was Peter, only a dark portrait against a vivid Colorado sunset, and here was another of Peter and Christy all tangled together as they had made their first attempts at cross-country skiing, while yet another showed Peter feeding a chipmunk while Christy was draped affectionately over his shoulder and their father watched in the background.

As she walked slowly past the wall, her breath was coming in gasps, and she openly sobbed. Why had her father done this? How could he stand, day after day, to see these reminders of what might have been? Sara had put away all her pictures of Peter along with her memories, and now only a small studio portrait of him taken by a professional photographer stood on her dresser. The picture was of a solemn Peter in his military uniform—bearable, because it wasn't really the Peter that she knew. She couldn't recall seeing any pictures of him in her father's house, and in fact once, several years ago, had asked her father if he had wanted a portrait like hers, and he had quickly shaken his head. And now here was this wall, almost a memorial to Peter. Of course, there were other photographs: studies of her mother and father, engaging portraits of Christy and innumerable pictures of mountains, flowers, birds and animals. But it was the pictures of Peter which drew her eyes to the exclusion of all others. She went back to the other end of the wall, and began looking at the photographs again, seeking out those of her brother, much as a thirsty man seeks water. At first, each picture sent a painful arrow to her heart, but gradually the photographs filled her with a sense of peace and thankfulness for the good times they had shared as a family. Slowly her sobbing quieted, and she wiped her hand across her face to brush away the tears, sniffing loudly.

Almost immediately a large white handkerchief was offered her, and without thinking, she grabbed it, muttered a 'thank you', and emphatically blew her nose. Only then did it dawn on her that hankies didn't just appear out of disembodied hands, and she spun quickly on her heels and saw Brad.

'Did you come in to pry?' She tried to snap out the words, but it was difficult when her voice was husky from crying, and she had to resort to blowing her nose again.

Brad didn't answer, but glanced at her, pity and disgust mingled in his eyes, then he discreetly walked away and looked at the photographs as she noisily blew her nose a third time.

She tried again. 'I should think you'd have better manners than to walk in on someone who obviously wanted to be private!'

Brad turned to look at her, one eyebrow raised quizzically. 'If you wanted to be private, you should have tried an empty room.' He indicated the antique wing chair in the corner, where an open newspaper offered mute testimony that someone had, indeed, been in residence.

'What are you doing here?' she blurted out, unable to contain the question any longer.

'I'm doing a crossword puzzle,' he answered lightly.

'You know that's not what I mean,' Sara stormed. 'Why are you here in Blanchard Valley?'

Brad seemed to be choosing his words. 'Your father invited me, and as the invitation was opportune, I decided to take advantage of it.' He hesitated. 'I thought you knew I was going to be here. It wasn't until yesterday that your father confessed that he hadn't informed you of my presence. He seemed to think you wouldn't show up if you knew.'

'He was right there,' Sara answered bitterly.

A spasm of anger crossed Brad's face, and he walked over to stare out of the window. 'Your father explained to me about the special relationship between you and Peter. He's concerned that after all these years you still haven't accepted Peter's death.'

'It's none of your business!'

'No, maybe it's not,' Brad said slowly, 'but I've grown fond of the Judge, and I hate to see him possibly risking his health worrying about you. It's time that you quit behaving like a spoiled brat who's wallowing in self-pity, angry because someone took your favourite toy away.'

'How dare you!' Sara cried. 'What a hateful thing to say! I loved Peter, and I miss him so much.' Stricken, the tears once again streamed down her face. A shaft of pain pierced her heart at Brad's cruel, yet perceptive, thrusts.

Brad swiftly crossed the room to her side and clasped her rigid shoulders. 'Sara, I'm aware that you think I'm an unfeeling brute to hassle you this way, but it's about time you faced up to life. Think about someone beside yourself, for a change.'

Sara could only shake her head helplessly at him, the tears raining down her face in torrents.

With an exasperated sigh, Brad abruptly enfolded her in his arms.

Still reeling from the impact of his punishing words, Sara clutched at his lapels and wept with abandon. Eventually her sobbing abated, and with deep gulping breaths, she tried to regain control. Spasms of unhappiness continued to shake her body. 'I'm making such a fool of myself,' she muttered. Embarrassment flamed her face at the sight of spreading patches of dampness on Brad's shirt front. She tried to withdraw from his encircling arms, but his clasp tightened.

'You and I ought to be able to deal together better than this,' he murmured into her hair.

The past ten years slipped from memory, and Sara weakly accepted Brad's embrace. So many times had she longed for this very moment, and she savoured its sweet intensity. Desire quivered through her body, and her lips longed to press against his. She raised her face.

'Are you ready to discuss this problem sensibly?' Brad's brisk words were a flood of icy water dashing her heated emotions.

Sara backed away from his arms. Her eyes refused to meet his. She concentrated on his mouth—white even teeth, firm moving lips. Her body swayed towards his, as if an invisible thread pulled her to him.

'Sara?' His hands gripped her shoulders, his thumbs pressing painfully.

Blood rushed to her head, warming her face, and she turned away. 'I didn't hear what you said,' she managed.

Brad frowned. 'I said we have to decide how we're going to handle this. There's your father's health to consider—in fact, it's the item of paramount importance. If my presence here this summer is going to cause tensions, I'll pack up and leave.'

'Yes,' Sara breathed. 'No!' Anguished, she sought support from Brad. 'I don't know,' she cried, wringing her hands.

Brad correctly read the appeal in her eyes. 'You want me to leave, but you don't want to distress your father.'

Dumbly, she nodded in agreement.

He strode up and down the room in silence for several moments, before turning back to face her. He rubbed his thumb roughly over her trembling lips. His touch shattered her, and she flinched away.

A cold look settled in his eyes. 'I'll leave after lunch,' he said abruptly. 'I can tell your father that something came up, and my leave has been cancelled.'

'Yes—no, you can't, Daddy ... Daddy wouldn't believe ... no message ... my fault ... we'll pretend, must think of Daddy ...' the disjointed phrases poured incoherently from Sara, until out of breath, she ran down.

'You want me to stay?' Brad asked in marked disbelief.

'No—yes. Not for me,' she added hastily. 'For the Judge. He seems to want you here. Surely we can keep out of each other's way?' her voice ended on a pleading note.

Brad's sharp eyes searched her face. 'Let's see if I understand you,' he said slowly. 'In view of your father's poor health, you're willing to put up with me this summer.'

'Yes.'

'Yes,' Brad mocked her bald answer. 'All right, I can go along with that. A truce, shall we say?' He extended his hand.

Unwillingly Sara slowly gave him hers. At his touch, a fiery dart ran up her arm. He pulled her near, but she guessed his purpose and jerked her hand away.

He uttered a low laugh, but let her go. 'Afraid?' he jeered.

She sniffed, refusing to answer. Maybe if she ignored him, he would go away. It was becoming more and more difficult to cope with his disturbing presence. She pretended a great interest in a picture of a dark blue stellar jay sitting on a snowy bough, but her ruse didn't work. Instead of feeling snubbed, Brad came closer to see the picture that merited such close scrutiny.

'Your father tells me that these pictures are all yours.' Sara nodded. 'I'm sure you're used to people saying that you do excellent work. I was amazed when your father told me that these were at least ten years old.'

She just shrugged. Why didn't he leave the room? If she left first, he'd think she was running away.

'I know your job has something to do with photography, but what exactly is it that you do?' Brad persisted.

Sara turned with the intention of telling him to leave her alone, then she saw that he was surveying her pictures with evident interest and admiration. 'I'm in commercial photography,' she finally admitted. 'To put it simply, I take pictures for a firm that puts out cookbooks, calendars, stationery and other paper items of that type.' She realised that Brad was demonstrating that if they were to spend the summer in close proximity, they would have to converse occasionally, and at least her work was a safe topic.

'Do you like what you're doing?'

'Yes, mostly I love my work. It's hectic, always deadlines to meet and so on, but I'm getting well paid for doing what I like to do best.'

'Why do you say "mostly" you love it?'

'Well,' Sara hesitated, 'I guess my first love is right here in Colorado, or at least, outdoors. I love the freedom of photographing what I want, when I want. There's a special thrill when I get a successful photo of a wild flower just as the morning sun lights up the dew, or the feeling of satisfaction from sitting all day to get that one perfect picture of an elusive bird.' She laughed ruefully. 'It probably sounds silly to you, but I love the challenge and spontaneity of nature photography that I simply don't find in a studio where I spend the day shooting still lifes of food and flowers.'

'Why don't you try freelancing?'

Sara went over to the window and gazed out with unseeing eyes at the lovely view. Almost to herself she said, 'I keep asking myself that. I guess I'm just a coward. I know I'm good at what I do now. I wish I had more time to do this sort of thing,' she turned and waved her hand at the wall of photographs, 'but I don't. Sometimes I promise myself I'll quit work and build up a portfolio, but it's such a risk. What if I'm not good enough, or if my style doesn't appeal to anyone?' She added in a lighter vein, 'A girl has to eat, you know!'

'Surely your father . . .'

'No,' she interrupted sharply. 'I'm a big girl now. I don't need anyone to take care of me with money or any other way.'

'I'll bet many men have offered,' Brad suggested.

Sara lowered her eyelids provocatively. 'I guess you could say I've had my chances.' Never would she let him know that the only man she had ever wanted to take care of her and to cherish her was Brad himself.

He eyed her curiously. 'Why didn't you take any of these "chances"?'

His question inspired Sara. Here was her opportunity to use Roger as a shield against Brad's magnetic personality. 'As a matter of fact,' she said carefully, 'I'm thinking about it now.'

A curious light flared in Brad's eyes. 'Oh? Your father didn't mention that.'

'I ... I haven't had the chance to tell him yet.' Guiltily she recalled that she had had plenty of opportunity while at breakfast, but she hadn't even remembered Roger's existence then.

'Tell me about this "chance".'

Sara shrugged. 'Not much to tell. Roger owns the agency where I work. We've grown used to each other, and ... and ... love each other,' she concluded defiantly. 'He's nice and handsome, and ... and ...'

'What a romantic tale!' Brad sneered.

'Yes, isn't it?' she countered sweetly.

'I'm curious as to why Roger let you leave him for a whole month. Or perhaps he's joining you later? A whole month without your lover must seem like an eternity.'

'He's not my ...' Sara stopped, aware that her unruly tongue had almost betrayed her. 'I'm not ... that is, Roger and I have a very open, trusting relationship, and we each feel free to do our own thing, and to come and go as we please,' she explained, choosing her words with painstaking care. 'Naturally, I miss Roger very much,' she said out loud, while inwardly her conscience felt a sharp nip at this patent untruth. She'd barely thought about Roger since her arrival in the Valley.

Brad shot her a doubtful look. 'Since coming to the Valley after all these years was bound to be an ordeal for you, it seems to me that this Roger should have come along to support you.'

'He wanted to,' Sara answered hotly, 'but it wasn't necessary. I can handle my own problems.'

'Yeah, I can see how great you've been doing on your own,' Brad said sarcastically. 'You can't convince me that you wouldn't like Roger here to hold your hand.'

'Oh, you men!' Sara said disdainfully. 'You're all alike—you think a woman can't exist without you.' She sought to turn Brad back from dangerous ground.

'Oh no!' He backed away in mock horror. 'Don't tell me you're one of these liberated women?'

'So what if I am? I seem to recall that the Armed Forces are doing a lot of shouting about their equal opportunities for men and women. Don't you believe in the "company policy"? I happen to believe in it, and I happen to like being independent.' Sara knew her voice was starting to reach the shouting stage, and she strove to speak more calmly. 'Age-old myths have no place in today's society, only men are afraid to admit that women are every bit as smart and as capable as they are. And, what's more . . .'

Christy provided a welcome diversion as she bounded into the room 'What are you two arguing about. I could hear Sara screaming!'

'I wasn't screaming,' Sara denied coolly, even as she breathed a sigh of relief at Christy's entrance.

'Says you,' Christy retorted. 'I could hear you hollering from six miles away!'

'Well then,' Sara giggled in spite of herself, 'you sure covered six miles in a hurry!'

Christy waved her hands airily. 'It's magic, that's all.'

'Brat.' Sara said affectionately. 'What do you want?'

'Really, Sara Louise,' Christy replied in a lofty tone, 'I don't think it's becoming to be called a brat when I've reached the advanced age of nineteen. The term "brat" seems to designate a grubby tomboyish urchin, and I don't think I qualify. Do you, Brad?' she asked in a wheedling voice as she tucked her arm under his.

Sara's heart lurched as Brad smiled down into her sister's lovely young face. Oh no! Don't let Christy fall for him like she had. History repeating itself would be more than she could bear. Sara seemed to hold her breath for Brad's reply.

'No,' he said consideringly, amusement written on his face. 'No, I don't think you're a grubby brat. I think you're a lovely young girl poised on the threshold of womanhood.'

'What do you mean, poised on the threshold?' Christy removed her arm from Brad's and faced him defiantly, eyes snapping. 'I *am* a woman!'

Sara tried in vain to stifle her giggle of relief, and Christy whirled to face her and shook her finger under Sara's nose. 'Don't you laugh at me, you—you ...' words failed her.

'Brat?' Sara suggested, then went into peals of laughter. Christy glared a minute and then laughed with her. Sara linked her arm with her sister's. 'Come on, woman,' she said, 'we've both been put down now, so let's march off together, showing him we're liberated women, and we don't care what a mere man thinks.' Ignoring Brad's protests, they laughingly left the room together. The mocking look on Brad's face told Sara that he recognised her exit for the headlong escape that it was.

The Judge met them in the hall, his countenance beaming. 'It's wonderful to hear laughter in this house again.' Impulsively he hugged both daughters to him and then gazed anxiously at Sara. 'You don't mind, then?'

'Mind what?' she asked cautiously.

'About the pictures,' the Judge explained. 'When I made a scouting trip several months ago to see what needed to be done up here, I couldn't abide the wall full of dead animals. Since Peter's death, hunting has lost its appeal for me, so I removed all the trophy heads, but I needed something to replace them with. I remembered all your boxes of slides, so I went through them to see if any would be suitable for framing and hanging up here. I picked out my favourites and had them enlarged.

I didn't mess up your order and I replaced everything as it was,' he reassured her quickly.

'But, Dad,' Sara protested in a horrified voice, 'what an awesome task. There must have been thousands of slides!'

'At least,' her father laughingly agreed. 'However, it wasn't a task at all. I enjoyed browsing through your work and reminding myself what a talented daughter I have. Oh, I must admit I was staggered when I saw the sheer number of the slides you had, but I had decided early on to limit my choice to photos taken here in the Valley. And I had help. Christy was home a number of times, and Mrs Collins spent many an evening helping me make my selections, and even Brad was there a time or two.'

'Brad? You showed all my slides to Brad?'

'All? I should say not! I said he was only there a time or two. I spent weeks viewing those slides. No, Brad was there when I was making those last hard eliminations. After all, I couldn't enlarge them all. Incidently, Brad was very impressed with your abilities.'

'I don't think I like the idea of strangers going through my personal slides, Dad.'

Her father looked at her oddly. 'I don't consider Brad a stranger, Sara.' He added slowly, 'I had anticipated that you might be upset at having a friend of Peter's here this summer, Sara, but I'm at a loss to understand this anger you seem to be directing at Brad.' Narrowed eyes surveyed her. 'You're a grown woman, Sara, and ordinarily I wouldn't presume to give you orders, but understand this—Brad is a guest in my house, and as far as I'm concerned, he's a very welcome guest.'

The tight rein that Sara had been holding on her emotions snapped. 'You're welcome to him!' she cried bitterly.

'Sara, I won't tolerate any discourtesy to a guest in this house,' her father admonished her sternly.

'I'll be civil, but don't expect anything more.' With this parting shot, Sara stomped up the stairs.

Her father let her get halfway up before his next words stopped her. 'Sara,' he said quietly, 'what if he were Peter? What if Peter had come back to no family? Wouldn't you want someone to take Peter into their home, their family, to give him their love? Sara,' he pleaded, 'I lost Peter, and Brad helped me bring him back—oh, not to life, but back into my life. I can remember Peter with love, not pain. All I'm asking is that you put away your inexplicable hostility towards Brad and behave like a decent human being towards him. It's only for one month. Surely that's not so much to ask?'

Sara remained motionless on the stairs as the sense of what her father was saying sunk in. She couldn't speak, and the tears coursed down her face.

'Sara!' her father shouted in exasperation. 'I'm just asking you to be nice to him! You don't have to fall in love!'

The word 'love' broke through Sara's distress, and she ran blindly up the stairs and into her room, slamming the door behind her.

Love him! she cried silently to the walls. Love him! I've already loved him once. The question is, does Brad know? Can I meet with him and talk to him every day without his realising my embarrassment and figuring out the cause? To him, I was nobody, just Peter's little sister. That's all I still am, she told herself, and wondered why she felt vaguely discontented.

She was in an awkward situation now, she mused. She had been younger than Christy was now when she had first fallen in love with Brad through his letters. She had been eighteen when he was released and had awaited his visiting her with youthful and eager anticipation. Then gradually it became apparent to her that she had meant nothing to Brad, as he had never materialised.

She had felt bereft in the beginning, and then angry

and disillusioned, until finally she had hated him with intensity. After a while, she had realised that her hate was just the other side of her love for Brad, and slowly, painfully, she had weaned herself until she had convinced herself that Brad had only been a teenage crush. The wounds had healed, and her heart had grown whole again.

And yet not really whole, she thought. Never again had she opened up her heart, her mind, her soul to someone as she had to Brad in her letters. She had poured out her very being to him, and maybe that was why she had had nothing left for other men. And there had been other men who had desired her—not thousands, but enough. She was intelligent and reasonably attractive. At this thought, Sara jumped up and peered into the mirror. Large hazel eyes with incredibly long black lashes stared back at her. Her skin was very fair, almost pale, but no artifice was needed to tint her rosy cheeks. Dark brown hair hung in waves to her shoulders. She remembered the picture that she had sent to Brad so long ago, a picture featuring two vivacious ponytails tied up with big bows, and a mouth full of teeth just free of braces. Freckles had marched across her nose, she recollected, and at the thought she leaned closer to the mirror. The freckles were fainter now, but she knew they were traitorously waiting for the Colorado sun to bring them forth in their brown shining glory. She grimaced at herself in the mirror. All in all, not too bad.

She wondered if Brad compared her looks now with that old picture. If only she could believe he regretted not coming for her eight years ago! He was nothing to her now, nothing at all. Still, it would somehow appease female vanity if she could think his presence in this valley was somehow linked with her own.

It was curious how he had never mentioned their letters, their only bond in the past. A disturbing thought momentarily shook Sara. Had Brad totally forgotten her? Did he even know who she was? Of course he did, she reminded herself. He had told her father about their correspondence. It was still odd, then, that he didn't say anything about the letters. Surely the natural thing would have been to mention them? She wasn't about to bring up the subject herself; it would be unbearable to have Brad put on an insincere show of gratitude for her letters.

Was he avoiding the subject because of guilt? Perhaps after all these years he was sorry for the rotten way he had treated her. Maybe meeting her father had triggered a desire to see Sara at long last. Was that why he was here? To say he was sorry? He didn't act apologetic. He acted more as if ... as if Sara didn't count, as if he didn't want to be friendly with her, but must because of Peter and her father. Her mind raced to find an explanation for Brad's presence here. Why was he here? It occurred to her that everyone seemed to evade the question. Suddenly it became very important that she find the answer.

The noon gong clanged loudly, and she realised that the sound had been a dim accompaniment to her thoughts for some minutes. Mentally she shook herself—Be sensible, be friendly and be pleasant. The month will pass. Quickly taking stock of her rumpled clothes, she tucked her shirt firmly into her shorts, tugged a comb through her long waves and made a pass over her lips with a touch of red. One last look in the mirror, an admonition to keep her chin up, and then resolutely she went down to lunch.

Halfway down the wide staircase, she saw the man in conversation with Brad and her father. 'Josh!' she screamed, and flew down the stairs two at a time and flung herself into the outstretched arms that awaited her. 'What are you doing here?' she demanded as she emerged for air after being thoroughly hugged and kissed.

'What I am doing here right this minute is starving to death because the lunch gong has been ringing for fifteen minutes now, and gentlemen that we are, we had to wait for a lady who's late as usual,' he teased.

'Oh, Josh,' Sara hugged him again, 'it's good to see you! What are you doing in this neck of the woods, anyway?'

'Didn't Christy tell you?' he asked in a surprised voice. 'I'm working at the dam construction site down the road. You'll have to get used to seeing me around, like it or not.'

'Looks to me as if she'll like it,' Brad observed dryly.

'Oh!' Sara hastily dropped Josh's arm. In her pleasure at seeing Josh she had forgotten the audience of Brad and her father. The next second she told herself she didn't care about Brad's opinion, and she gaily linked her hands with her father and Josh and steered them towards the dining room. 'C'mon, you guys, lead me to the food! You, too, Colonel,' she called over her shoulder. 'With Josh here, we'll all have to dig in fast if we want to get any food!'

'Yes, ma'am,' he solemnly saluted her and followed the three into the dining room.

As Sara was biting into a luscious hunk of watermelon, she covertly watched Josh while he lightheartedly teased her sister. Christy bloomed under his attention and managed to hold her own in the repartee. Little sister is growing up, thought Sara in surprise. Wouldn't it be wonderful if Christy and Josh made a twosome? Josh was Sara's age and not too old for Christy. She frowned with concentration trying to decide how to promote this intriguing idea.

'Jealous?' a soft whisper tickled her ear, and she turned to see Brad, who sat on her right, looking at her with speculative eyes.

'Jealous?' she asked, astonished. 'Of whom?'

Brad nodded across the table to where Christy was engrossed in a humorous story that Josh was relating to the Judge. 'It looks like Christy is out to steal your other boy-friend.'

Sara let out a spontaneous peal of laughter. 'Josh? Don't be ridiculous! He's not my boy-friend.'

Brad raised a sceptical eyebrow. 'He received a

mighty warm welcome for a casual acquaintance. What would Roger think? Lucky you have such a trusting relationship. Is Josh the reason you didn't want Roger to come out here with you?'

'I didn't say Josh was a casual acquaintance,' Sara replied, ignoring the latter jabbing remarks. 'He's the son of Dad's old law partner. I've known him practically all my life, he's like my second brother. His mother died when he was young, and Josh just naturally spent his vacations with us. Now he thinks of us as his family, and that's the way we want it.'

At that moment Josh finished his story and turned to Sara down the table. 'What are you two whispering about?' he demanded to know.

'Nothing important. Just you,' Sara retorted.

'Thanks heaps! What a thing for a feller's best girl to say about him!' He broadly winked at Sara before Christy reclaimed his attention.

'A brother, huh?' Brad questioned wryly.

Sara knew she was blushing furiously. 'Josh is always teasing. Why, I might just as well say that you were my boy-friend, and then . . .' she stopped abruptly as she realised where her unwary tongue was leading her. 'Have some more watermelon,' she said as she blindly shoved the bowl of fruit at Brad.

'That's a good idea,' he agreed blandly.

Startled, she stared at him. 'What's . . . what's a good idea?' she stuttered.

'Why, having some more watermelon,' he answered as he helped himself to several large chunks. There was no doubt about the amusement on his face as he asked politely. 'What else could I have meant?'

'Never mind,' Sara muttered, and she concentrated very hard on picking seeds from her watermelon. It was going to be a long month indeed!

She looked down the long table, watching Josh and her father speaking animatedly to each other. She hadn't seen Josh in over a year, and now she looked him over as if he were a stranger. He was an attractive man with his curly red hair that was always a mess from his running his hands wildly through it as he talked. Mrs Collins said his smile was enough to charm the birds from the trees, and it had certainly charmed many a cookie from the housekeeper in their childhood. His blue eyes sparkled with fun behind small glasses that he was constantly pushing back up his nose. She hadn't seen his beard before, red and bushy, and she thought it gave him a jolly Santa Claus air, which was probably not the image that he sought.

Christy sat, chin in hand, her fork only now and again successfully gathering food and finding its way to her mouth. She was clearly fascinated by Josh and hung on his every word, which decided Sara to try and discover Josh's feelings for her sister, because to her mind they would make a perfect match.

After lunch Josh returned to work following a loud and hectic farewell. Sara dropped down laughing on to the veranda. 'I always feel like I've been through a hurricane when Josh is around,' she confided to her father.

The Judge laughed in agreement. 'Yes, Josh is what we used to call a real live-wire. It's refreshing having him around, but relaxing when he leaves. It's a good thing that he chose an outdoor career where he can expend some of those energies.'

Sara giggled. 'Can you picture Josh in a business suit pleading a case in court, like his father wanted?'

The Judge chuckled. 'I doubt the judicial scene realises how close a call they had. Fortunately, Josh chose his own path in life, and he's an excellent engineer.'

'I think Josh would be a success at whatever he tried,' Christy defended him hotly.

The Judge winked at Sara over Christy's head. 'I'm sure you're right, dear,' he said in a conciliatory tone.

Christy refused to be appeased. 'Josh is a fine person, and I don't like to hear you make fun of him.'

'My dear Christy,' the Judge said in distress, 'I'm not

making fun of Josh. I love him dearly, and I'm sure he doesn't require a heated testimonial from anyone to prove his great worth to me.'

'I just think we should appreciate him more, if you know what I mean,' Christy muttered.

Sara observed her sister's high colour before drawling, 'Yes, I think I do know what you mean. Do you see Josh much in Denver?' she asked in a casual voice.

'Oh, now and again,' Christy answered in a voice as carefully casual. 'Of course,' she added fairly, 'we mostly talk about you.'

'Me?' Sara squeaked.

'Well, yes. I mean, you two are kind of a "thing", aren't you?'

'We are not,' Sara denied firmly. 'Josh and I are very close friends, but there's nothing romantic between us at all.'

'There's not?' Christy looked blissfully happy for one second, then added carelessly, 'Not that I care, of course.'

'Of course not,' Sara agreed. She got up and crossed the veranda, turning just as she reached the door. 'Christy,' she called softly.

'Hmm?' Christy turned to look up at her.

'You can have Josh with my blessing,' said Sara as she quickly left the veranda to evade the pillow that Christy threw at her.

The hall was dark after the brightness outside, momentarily blinding her. Smiling to herself, she didn't see the large body that abruptly halted her progress.

'Hey, do you always come into this hall like a windstorm? Every time I've seen you, you've come in here on the run!'

Sara blinked a couple of times, and Brad's face came into focus. 'Oh, I'm sorry,' she said, confusion overcoming her as she felt his arms around her steadying her. 'I didn't see you. The sun ...' she gestured vaguely towards the outside door.

'Boy-friend gone?' Brad enquired.

'He's not my boy-friend!' she snapped as she stamped her foot in vexation. 'I wish everyone would quit saying that!'

'Everyone?' He looked out on the veranda and spotted Christy before adding in a commiserating tone, 'Oh, Christy is worried about cutting you out of the picture. She wouldn't want to steal her sister's boy-friend.'

Sara looked at him in amazement. 'You're right. But why she should think Josh and I are a twosome is beyond me.'

'Maybe it's because she saw your loving greeting to Josh and heard Josh call you his favourite girl-friend.'

Sara frowned. 'Those things don't mean anything. I'll just have to come up with some way to convince her that Josh and I are only good friends.'

'Tell her you already have a boy-friend.'

'Sure, but who?'

'How about Roger?' Brad asked dryly.

Sara squirmed under Brad's intent scrutiny. 'She might not believe that. After all, she's never heard of him—that is to say,' she hastily corrected herself, 'she's never met him.'

'I have a better idea, then.'

'What?'

'You could pretend you're in love with me.'

Aghast, Sara stared at him. Then her heart skipped a beat. Was Brad serious? No, he was grinning at her. She grimaced at him. 'No, thanks, I'm not that desperate.' She turned to go upstairs.

Brad grabbed at her wrist and pulled her back. 'It might be fun, even more fun than being a liberated woman who doesn't need a man. At one time we appeared to be on the same wavelength.'

His oblique reference to their correspondence startled Sara, but she couldn't let him know. Pretending to think over his idea, she screwed up her face in exaggerated concentration. 'Nope,' she answered at last.

'Too boring. I have better things to do on my summer vacation.'

'Do you now?' Brad murmured, and before she had guessed his intention, he had tightened his grip and pulled her body towards him. Keeping her wrist in one hand, he placed his other hand on the back of her head and firmly brought her face up to his.

Sara knew she ought to struggle, but her bones were turned to jelly. I need willpower, she thought wildly as his lips sought, and successfully captured, hers. She felt his arm around her waist, and discovered her arms were free and had crept up Brad's chest and were now grasping the back of his neck, as if to prevent him from removing his lips from hers. She had been kissed many times, kisses that ranged from inept to smoothly professional, but never had she felt this fire in her stomach, this weakness in her legs that forced her to lean even more against Brad. His lips forced hers to part, then she heard herself moan in disappointment when he abandoned her lips, only to gasp with pleasure as he nibbled her earlobes and then trailed kisses down the side of her face. He positioned her head to rest against his shoulder, and she sighed in contentment as his lips found the pulse at the base of her throat. In seconds she knew contentment was not what she felt, and her lips sought his, demanding that he once again plunder their depths. In the back of her mind, she heard Brad give a quiet chuckle, but she was too busy answering kiss with kiss to heed. After some minutes of pressing her body into his, loud sounds from outside penetrated her dazed mind, and almost at the same moment Brad slowly thrust her away.

'Well, well,' he drawled in amusement as she tried to blink the passion from her eyes, 'do you still think it would be too boring?'

The sound of voices on the veranda snapped Sara out of her somnolent state. 'Definitely!' she retorted, her mind reeling crazily. How dared Brad behave as if he had only to snap his fingers and she would once more

be his toy, his diversion! The kisses that they had just
shared had meant nothing to him. Worse still, he was
well aware of their devastating effect on her and dared
to laugh at her. Turning on her heels, she marched
outside.

'Ces!' She stopped in amazement. 'What are you
doing here?'

'Darling, you invited me.'

CHAPTER THREE

STUNNED, Sara stared at the beautiful woman who had obviously just driven up. She was tall, with honey-blonde hair worn coiled low on the nape of her neck and blue eyes that surveyed the world coolly from beneath heavy dark brows. Her mouth featured a full sensuous lower lip that made her appear in a perpetual pout and promised a sultry siren that was at total variance with her untouchable personality. As usual, Ces was clothed in casual elegance from the top of her well-groomed head past a creamy-coloured silk shirt tucked into close-fitting designer jeans to expensive leather moccasins on her feet. Perfectly applied make-up set off a tan carefully acquired with the judicious use of a sun lamp.

'Have you quite finished looking me over?' Ces drawled with an uplifted eyebrow. 'Perhaps you didn't mean that invitation after all.' Her pout grew more pronounced.

'Ces, of course you're always welcome here. Sara's just surprised to see you,' the Judge spoke hastily.

Although Sara had not really meant the carelessly issued invitation to her room-mate, she endeavoured to sound enthusiastic. 'Of course you're welcome here. But why are you here? When I invited you, you snorted and said no way would you bury yourself in the country this summer—and besides, I thought you had several assignments on your calendar.'

'Darling, I never snort,' Ces said in reproof. 'The answer to your question is really too depressing. Would you believe that with all the care I take of my health and body, I picked up a bug from some silly technician. Oh, nothing serious, a mild strep throat—but, my dear, it really panicked me to think a germ could lay me low.

49

I decided I must be tired and overworked, so I reconsidered your invitation, cancelled all my assignments, and here I am to lie in the sun and regenerate. Surely you understand?'

Sara did understand. Ces was a fanatic about caring for herself. After all, Sara admitted to herself, that lovely body supported Ces pretty well. In return, Ces strictly controlled her diet, swallowed a heavy daily dose of vitamins, exercised dutifully one hour a day, and thrice weekly spent time at a near-by health spa, never smoked, never drank, and was always early to bed. Even the handsomest, most ardent suitor couldn't keep Ces up past her self-imposed bedtime. Sara could imagine the horror Ces had felt when it seemed her body had betrayed her. She had frequently seen Ces carefully scrutinising her face and body for the tiniest wrinkle or the faintest bulge that might spell finish to her career. Sara shuddered at the amount of time and devotion that kept Ces near the peak of perfection and at the top of her field as a model.

Ces had been chatting with Christy and the Judge, but now her eyes widened as she gazed over Sara's shoulder. 'Perhaps I should have called ahead. I didn't realise you already had a house guest,' she said smoothly.

Sara knew without turning that Brad had stepped through the door on to the veranda behind her.

Her father performed the introductions. 'Brad, this is Cecilia Saunders. Somewhere along the line we're related, making Ces some sort of distant cousin. Ces, this is James Bradley Rawlins. Colonel Rawlins, or Brad, was a close friend of Peter's.'

Ces elegantly extended her hand.

'Like royalty,' Christy sniffed into Sara's ear.

'Cease?' Brad enquired as he took the proffered hand.

'C-E-S, even if it is pronounced "cease" as in "cease fire," ' Ces stated coolly. 'The letters are my initials. My family has always called me Ces for short.'

'Cecilia Saunders,' Brad mused, still holding Ces'
hand. 'And the E stands for?'

Ces regained her hand. 'How long will you be
visiting, Colonel? I wouldn't want to put you out of
your room.'

'No problem there,' the Judge intervened. 'Brad is off
in the guest cabin. He needs the peace and privacy.'

'How fascinating! You must tell me why some time,
and all about yourself.' Ces stepped up to Brad and
looked wide-eyed into his face.

Sara thought Brad looked as if he'd been hit by a
truck. Disgustedly she turned to go into the house.

'Edna!' Christy intoned loudly.

Ces turned angrily red and hissed at Christy, 'Be
quiet!'

Brad looked confused. 'Edna?' he asked.

Christy shot a wicked look at Ces. 'I guess Ces didn't
hear your question about what the E stands for. The E is
for Edna.'

'Christy——' Ces began warningly.

The younger girl continued, undaunted. 'Cecilia Edna
Saunders,' she chanted. 'We used to call her that when
we were younger. It absolutely made her livid! Finally
Daddy made us quit, so we compromised on Ces. Ces
thinks it sounds elegant, but to the rest of us, it reminds
us of her mom yelling "Cecilia Edna Saunders!"
whenever she was naughty.' Christy grinned mischievously at Ces.

'Why, you little ...' Ces gritted between clenched
teeth.

'Here, Ces,' Sara interrupted hurriedly, 'I'll help you
carry in your stuff—Christy, you run and tell Mrs
Collins that Ces is here.'

Christy disappeared into the house with a gay flip of
her head.

'I'm sorry, Ces,' the Judge apologised. 'That was
inexcusable of Christy. I don't know what got into her.'

'She's always been spoiled rotten!' snapped Ces.
Then she remembered Brad standing near her bemused

by the conversation, and she laughed lightly. 'Children,' she said in a dismissing tone. 'Christy never did like me. I always thought she was jealous because you and I have always been so close, Judge.' She linked her arm in his. 'I'm famished after that long drive. Lead me to a nice cool drink and food!'

The Judge gravely escorted her inside. 'Did you drive all the way here alone, my dear?'

'Heavens, no,' Ces trilled. 'I flew into Aspen and rented a car. Someone will have to return it tomorrow. Sara,' she tossed over her shoulder, 'be a dear and carry in my bags—I'm exhausted!' She smiled demurely at Brad. 'Coming, Colonel?'

'In a minute,' he assented.

'Well, Colonel,' said Sara with a saccharine emphasis on his title, 'you look like you've been hit by an atom bomb.' Inwardly she fumed to think he could kiss her as he did and show no sign of being affected at all, and then be so overwhelmed by the mere presence of Ces. 'Don't you think you'd better go have a drink with them, to help you recover?'

Brad grinned. 'She is pretty high-powered, I'll have to admit—however, I think I'm sufficiently recovered to carry in her baggage.'

Sara leaned against the side of the car as he reached in and grabbed the keys from the ignition, then opened the car boot. 'Brad,' she asked curiously, 'why do you need peace and quiet? I've been wondering why you're off in the cabin by yourself when there's plenty of room in the big house.'

'Are you missing me?' Brad leered comically at her.

'Desperately!' Sara mocked, her hand placed dramatically over her heart.

'I'll bet,' he muttered. He pulled out six suitcases. 'I wouldn't have believed all this would fit in this little car. Is she here for the entire summer?'

'Ces always travels well equipped,' Sara agreed. 'You haven't answered my question about peace and quiet, Brad,' she went on determinedly. 'Are you ill, too?'

'Actually,' he leaned against the side of the car beside her and stared off towards the mountains, 'I'm writing a book.'

'A book?' Whatever Sara had expected him to say, it wasn't this.

'Memories just got to be too much for me, Sara, so I finally wrote them all down. My commanding officer is a former P.O.W. as well, and we talked about it, then he asked to read what I'd written. Unknown to me, he sent the material off to an old friend of his in the publishing business. Even after all these years, the war in Vietnam is still raising headlines of one type or another, and this publisher wants my book.'

Sara didn't know what to say. A book—Brad was writing a book!

He continued, 'I didn't want to publish the book. It's not a book really, just a series of anecdotes about people and a lot of how I felt about things. It was a catharsis for me, Sara. Once I'd written all these feelings down in black and white, I was better able to live with and accept my memories. That's also how I got started with the few speeches that I gave. My C.O. and this publisher convinced me that the general public ought to hear what we who had suffered had felt about this war that affected us all in this country so drastically.'

Sara slowly nodded. 'And Peter—is Peter in your book?' she asked in a low voice.

'Yes,' Brad answered quietly. 'But not exploited, Sara. Your dad read the book, and he didn't mind. Sara, please,' he tilted her chin up and looked steadily into her eyes. 'You're Peter's sister, and out of memory of him, I wouldn't intentionally hurt you, but this book is very important to me. If the thought of the book or its contents upsets you . . .' He shrugged. 'I have to do this, with or without your understanding.' His voice trailed off as he awaited her reply.

Sara stared at this man who had meant so much to her so many years ago. She saw the grey hair which had so shocked her, the scars, the lines for ever etched in his face by untold pain and suffering, the slight tremor in his cheek, the lips which so recently had kissed her now clenched tight, and she saw the resolute purpose in his eyes. However much she had been hurt by Brad, he had obviously suffered tenfold in the prison camp. She had no right to try and deny him his healing process. Sorrow and compassion rose in her throat, choking off any attempts at speech.

At her silence, Brad dropped his hand from her chin and turned to pick up the luggage.

Pity shot painfully through her heart as she saw the dejected slump of his shoulders. 'Brad,' she said softly, 'not now, but some day, I'd like to read your book.'

'Sara!' He dropped the luggage and turning, hugged her to him. 'Thank you,' he said as he kissed her lightly on her forehead. 'You're a kind person, Sara Blanchard.'

Embarrassed by his words, and shaken by his nearness, she shrugged off his hands and moved over to pick up a small tote bag belonging to Ces. 'Brad, if your book has already been accepted, what are you writing now?'

'It was accepted,' he acknowledged with a grimace, 'but the publisher wanted a few minor changes, and I'm working on that and trying to pull all the various sketches into a coherent whole. I took two months' leave with the blessings of my superiors so I could get this over and done with once and for all.'

'Hey, you two, what are you plotting out there?' Christy bounced cheerfully out of the door. 'Her Majesty says get a hustle on with those bags. The hot sun could be devastating to her bottles of make-up,' she sarcastically mimicked Ces's cool lofty tones.

Brad clicked his heels together and smartly saluted Christy. 'I hear and rush to obey, General.' He swiftly hauled up the two largest pieces and a garment bag and headed in through the door.

Christy giggled. 'Silly—as if I were the one issuing

orders around here! Ces is the one who wants to be treated as royalty. I don't see how you stand to live with her.'

Sara shrugged. 'Alone, we couldn't afford an apartment near as nice as we can with two of us sharing the rent. Actually, we barely see each other.' She turned troubled eyes on her mischievous younger sister. 'Christy, I hope you aren't going to start off by antagonising Ces—as usual, I might add.'

'Why did Ces have to butt in here where she's not wanted? How dumb can you be to invite her out here?' Christy hooted when she saw Sara's face turn bright red. 'You only invited her because you thought she'd never come. Serves you right! But what about me? I'd planned such a cosy summer, just you and me and Dad. First Josh and Brad show up—not that I mind them,' she added generously, 'Brad's a dream, and we seldom see him anyway as he's always off writing that horrid book.'

'What do you mean by horrid?' Sara asked apprehensively. 'Have you read it?'

'Well, no,' Christy admitted. 'Not all of it, but I did read a part where he talks about Peter.'

Sara caught her breath. 'You read something about Peter, and it was horrid?' Her mind chilled.

'Maybe not horrid, but definitely sickening. Blood and guts and all that, you know,' said Christy candidly, showing little emotion.

'Christy——' Sara hesitated, 'do you miss Peter at all?'

'Oh, sure.' Christy paused. 'Well, not like you do, Sara. After all, I was only nine when he went away. I mean, I was just a little kid to him, and we didn't do much together. It wasn't like with you and him . . .' Her voice trailed off apologetically.

After a moment of embarrassed silence, Christy asked in a small voice. 'Will it be okay for you this summer, Sara?'

'What do you mean?'

'I know how you still grieve for Peter. I personally don't think it's healthy, and Dr Scott said——' Christy faltered.

'Dr Scott?'

'My psychology instructor at the University.'

Sara heaved a dramatic sigh. 'Christy Ann Blanchard, I do not need any warmed-over psychology from your first-year psychology class! Is that clear?' she asked sharply.

Christy continued to look at her with clear young eyes. 'Sara, I just wanted you to know I do understand, and if everyone here, Brad and Ces, and even Josh, gets to you, you can always come to me for comfort,' she finished stolidly.

The thought of going to her baby sister for comfort almost made Sara laugh out loud, until she realised that Christy was serious and would be crushed at being mocked. Impulsively she hugged her. 'Thanks, I will,' she muttered in a smothered voice.

'That's that, then.' Christy was obviously nonplussed by Sara's demonstration of affection, and to hide her confusion she marched over to Ces's luggage. 'I don't care if this sits out here until next week, but Dad told me to shape up, so I guess I'll have to carry some in to try and make amends.' She shouldered a tote bag and a make-up case.

'Here, I'll help,' offered Sara, and picked up the remaining case and a couple of parcels.

Christy giggled. 'I brought one suitcase and a knapsack. All this makes me feel like I ought to go shopping tomorrow!'

Sara laughed. 'I know how you feel. When Ces and I first began living together, I blew every bit of my salary on clothes and make-up. I finally realised that Ces is Ces, and Sara is Sara, and I'd just better stick with what little I've got.'

Christy inspected Sara's long lean legs and the lovely curves enchanced by the yellow top. 'I think what little you've got is sufficient,' she observed dryly.

'Thank you, kind lady,' Sara dimpled, and dropped a curtsy as low as her burdens would allow. 'You're not so bad yourself, with those gorgeous tan legs a mile long beneath indecent short shorts. And I must say, that tee-shirt does little to hide your charms.'

'Yup,' Christy assented, 'I've always been happy I developed like you.' The two sisters grinned at each other.

'What is this, a mutual admiration society?' Brad stood on the porch, legs apart, hands on his hips. 'I do all the work while you two stand around and admire each other's legs!' He assumed a lecherous sneer. 'My dears, you carry in the luggage, and I'll admire your legs.'

Sara felt her face warm up and knew that she was fiery red as she realised Brad had been standing there some minutes listening to her and Christy's absurd conversation.

Christy, however, was totally in command, and she boldly raked Brad's body with her eyes. 'Your legs are pretty good, too,' she assessed slyly. 'They look strong, too, like your back,' and with meaning, she handed him two of her heaviest bags.

Brad laughed and disappeared through the back door again.

Christy waited for Sara to climb the veranda stairs and then whispered dramatically, 'Brad is so nice. We must save him from Cecilia Edna.'

Sara stiffened. 'I doubt Brad needs saving from a beautiful woman.'

Casting back a scornful look, Christy marched off into the house after Brad. Her last words floated back to Sara. 'You're dumb, Sara!'

Sara remained by the car, deep in thought. So there was a simple explanation for Brad's presence here after all. He needed the privacy to write his book, and as he had said earlier, her father's invitation had been opportune. No doubt everyone had hedged around his reason for being here because they feared that Brad's book would disturb her.

Her heart dropped to her toes. Until that moment she hadn't realised how much she had hoped that Brad was there on her account. But no, he had not sought her out. As far as he was concerned, her being there was incidental. Christy was right, she thought bitterly. She was dumb.

Dumb. The word returned to Sara's thoughts a week later as she lay on her back in a secluded glen near the river, thoughtfully chewing on a blade of grass. It wasn't Sara who was dumb. It was Brad. All her resolutions to be nice to Brad were scarcely needed as they barely saw each other. Ces saw to that.

To his credit, Brad was busy at work. Her bedroom window faced his cabin, and she knew he was working doggedly at his typing every day. Mrs Collins delivered him his breakfast and lunch when he didn't cook his own, but he joined the family at dinner. To the Judge's queries, Brad always said the book was 'coming along'.

With Sara, his encounters established a cool superficial tone, as if to remind her that he only tolerated her for her father's sake. Ces appropriated his free time and his arm, treating him with a possessive air which appeared to suit Brad very much. Sara refused to analyse why this irritated her so much.

To Sara's delight, Christy and Josh grew closer together without any help from her, and were obviously in love. Josh joined them every night for dinner, and then he and Christy hit the local bright spots or stayed by the fire to bicker amicably over a card game.

Ces, having confiscated Brad, made it quite clear that Sara was not welcome to join their twosome. Sara had been secretly amused the first night when Brad had suggested a moonlight stroll to the whole room. Josh and Christy had accepted with alacrity, while Ces had fumed. Sara had refused Brad's invitation and chosen to remain behind with the Judge. Christy had gleefully described the walk later to Sara, telling of Ces's manifest terror of the dark with a howling coyote sending her hot-footed back to the lodge. Thereafter Ces had worn long skirts and high heels to dinner. The Judge had commented on how lovely and elegant she looked, with an askance look at his jean-clad daughters. They both grinned, knowing Ces's apparel had been chosen to prevent further evening walks. The manoeuvre proved successful. Some evenings Ces had gone to Brad's cabin for a drink. True, he had invited everyone, but in the face of Ces's obvious disapproval, they always all declined.

One evening as Sara lay awake in the dark, she had heard Ces's and Brad's voices, and lost to all shame had crept to her window. Kneeling on the floor, she had peeped over the sill in time to see Brad escorting Ces back to the lodge. Her spying act had been rewarded by the sight of Ces melting into Brad's arms. Sara didn't wait around for the duration of what she felt sure would be a prolonged love scene and tiptoed weakly back to bed, disgusted at her interest.

She had to admit to herself that the evenings were growing longer and longer. She had anticipated fun and games by the fireplace with just her, her father and Christy. Instead, she was forced to watch Ces on the prowl with Brad the willing victim and see Josh and Christy lost in their private world. A couple of evenings she and the Judge had played chess, but he usually went to bed early, forcing her to play the fifth wheel or retire to her room and read. She told herself she didn't care, but still thought it would be nice if someone noticed her once in a while.

The days were lovely. Sara was up early each morning for a quick breakfast and then off outdoors. Camera in hand, she hiked the Valley that she loved and knew so well. The lovely columbine, Colorado's state flower, was at the height of its summer glory now, and she shot numerous rolls of film capturing the flower in all its shades of blue from almost white to the deepest violet. One morning she had happened on a doe with her fawn, appealing in its spotted coat and bouncy gait.

Crimson Indian paintbrush and lavender showy daisies had posed in glorious splendour for her camera's eye. She had snapped the engaging chickadee as he had hopped the trees along the trails. A grey jay had boldly flown in for a treat and skittered away at the camera's click. Chipmunks and ground squirrels eyed her as curiously as she eyed them, until finally they went about their daily business, ignoring her and her camera. One day she had placed food in hats, mittens, an old teapot. and even a snowboot, and could scarcely contain her amusement enough to photograph the chipmunks' entertaining antics as they discovered and robbed the hidden caches of food.

She discovered a lovely field of blue columbine that defied all her efforts to capture its breathtaking beauty, until in desperation she dragged Ces to the field where she photographed her in a filmy lavender dress that danced like the flowers in the summer breeze and emphasised their fragile colours. One morning Christy had appeared at breakfast in a sunny yellow playsuit, and before she had even finished her coffee, Sara had her sitting in a field of sunflowers, the yellows all combining to give an aura of sunny innocence. Even her father had not been safe from her as she posed him in his loudly checked lumberman's shirt, a pipe she had picked up at the local drug store clenched firmly in his teeth, as he leaned against a rustic old stock fence. She arose early and shot the first rays of the sun rosy on the mountain peaks, and photographed the peaks fiery red at sunset. White fluffy clouds and rain-streaked skies were images she felt compelled to capture. She was striving to illustrate the essence, the purity and the beauty of her valley and the mountains surrounding it. She wanted to put on a film a statement of her love for this very special place.

Lying there now in the sun she felt good about what she had done. Perhaps she could sell some of her prints, and begin to do a little freelance work, or at least begin on a portfolio.

Sara was lying on a huge flat rock beside the noisy rushing stream. She had arisen very early and hiked up to the ridgeline to search out alpine flowers and had been in rapture at the abundance of alpine forget-me-nots and deer clover. The tiny flowers had presented technical problems that had strained her knowledge, but with a great deal of experimentation, she was satisfied at least some of her shots should be good, if not terrific. Tired and contented, while hiking home, she had also been hot, and had remembered this rock from summers past.

Reclining now on the rock, she remembered how in years past it had served as castle, ocean liner, lookout tower, cavalry fortress and whatever else fertile imaginations could devise. Beneath the rock several other rocks jutted out into the sparkling water and created a small deep backwater pool which lay cool and tranquil, oblivious to the rushing water around it. Peter and Sara had called this pool their swimming hole, and when the river had calmed after the spring run-off, they had enjoyed hours of cooling fun there.

With the sun beating down on her, Sara felt hot and sweaty from her arduous hike. The thought of the refreshing water below her drew her like a magnet, and she rolled over on to her stomach and stretched her length across the huge rock to dangle her hand in the water. An idea burst into her head. She quickly rolled over again and sat up, looking carefully around her. No one was in sight or likely to be. Christy had gone off for the day with Josh. Her father didn't hike this far any more, and Ces certainly wouldn't risk an ankle on the steep twisty trail that led to this place, even if she could find it. Brad, of course, would be working.

Once thought of, the idea gave her no peace. She unlaced her heavy trail boots, removed the red wool socks and the thin white ones beneath and thrust her feet into the cool tangy water. Instant refresher! She stood up on the rock. Her jeans dropped to the ground, followed by her red gingham blouse. A quick glance around, and then her underwear joined the pile. The thought came to her that if she had left it on, she would be more covered than Ces had been yesterday out tanning in her skimpy bikini.

Sara carefully worked her way down to the water's edge and gingerly dipped a toe into the pool and quickly removed it. This is no way to get into the water hole, she scolded herself firmly. It requires tradition. She scrambled back up on the rock smiling at her foolishness. She and Peter had always made an offering to the river to appease the mountain gods. Now with her arms raised high, her breasts heaving from the exertion of climbing up the rock, and lifting her face to the mountains, she intoned loudly, 'Gods of the high places, I give you a virgin!' Then, shrieking, 'Geronimo!' she jumped wildly into the pool. The shock of the icy cold water took her breath away.

The second shock was the voice from the rock. 'You probably gave at least a dozen fish heart attacks. If fish can have heart attacks, that is,' the voice teased.

Stunned, Sara looked up to see Brad standing on the rock above her. Remembering her state of undress, she ducked further under the water. 'What are you doing here?'

'Saving virgins,' he chuckled.

'Oh,' Sara blushed. 'How long have you been spying on me?'

'Spying?' Brad raised a sardonic eyebrow. 'You didn't seem to be so private, shouting to the whole valley that you're still a virgin.'

Sara wondered if she should just sink under the water and drown right here and now. It would certainly be a cold death. In spite of herself, her teeth chattered.

'That pool must be freezing,' said Brad. 'Come out of there.'

'Not until you go away,' Sara said crossly.

'I'm not going away until you come out.'

'Then I stay here,' she said rebelliously.

Brad lay down on the rock, positioning his head

comfortably on his arms. 'That's all right with me. I'm nice and warm in the sun.'

Sara made a sound.

'Did you say something,' he asked with spurious interest.

'I was merely gritting my teeth.'

'Enjoying your swim?' he asked in amusement.

'Go away!' Sara was beginning to feel numb, and she was sure her skin was an unbecoming shade of blue.

'Be a good girl and come out,' Brad coaxed.

'I'd rather freeze,' she said disdainfully.

'My, my, such hostility! Have I offended you?' he asked with mock concern.

'Go away!' Sara's teeth chattered loudly.

'Say please,' Brad instructed.

'Brad, please be a gentleman and go away,' Sara pleaded, looking up at him beseechingly. 'Please, Brad,' she begged again in a soft voice.

He stared at her a minute. 'I'll start on down the trail. If you haven't caught up with me in five minutes, I'll be back,' he added in a no-compromise voice.

'Yes, Brad,' she acquiesced through teeth clenched against the cold.

Brad stood up and without a backward glance took off down the trail. He began whistling loudly a popular tune. Sara grinned as she realised the whistle was his way of letting her know he was keeping his word and leaving the area.

She was definitely feeling the effects of the cold water now, and she swam over to the stepping stones which led out of the pool. Her brow wrinkled as the stones were not where she remembered. Curious at first, and then with mounting panic, she swam round and round the pool. She couldn't find them. It was impossible to climb up the rocks of the three upsteam sides of the pool as they were too steep and slippery with moss. The fourth side of the pool offered no escape either. To go that way would put her in the midst of the torrent raging down from the mountains, and even in midsummer, it would be too strong a current for her in a normal state. It would be tantamount to suicide to try to fight the current in her present cold, numbed state. A sob caught in her throat, and she yelled for Brad to come back. Treading water, she waited in vain for his answer. He must have gone too far down the trail to hear her.

Terrified now, she tried to claw her way back up the slick rocks, but again and again she fell back into the water. Her hands were white and wrinkled from the cold. Her toes, knees and fingers were skinned from grappling with the rough slimy rocks, but the cold water had washed them clean. At least she wouldn't die of tetanus, she thought crazily as she gave up her efforts and barely managed to float. Her eyelids grew heavy, flickered, and began to shut.

'Sara! Sara, wake up!' The demanding voice forced her to open her eyes.

'Brad!' she breathed thankfully. 'I knew you'd be back.'

'You idiot! Why are you still in there?'

'Don't yell at me.' Sara started to cry. 'It's not my fault,' she protested. 'The stepping stones are gone—I can't get out.'

'Swim over by me and raise your arms up as high as you can,' Brad briskly instructed.

She did as he ordered and felt him grip her wrists and then haul her slowly up. She winced as the rock scratched her tender skin. Suddenly Brad gave a mighty tug, and using her toes to help, Sara scrambled up the rock sides and collapsed in a heap on top of him.

'You stupid idiot!' Brad fumed. 'I can't believe you didn't check before you leaped madly into the water. Why didn't you?'

'It's traditional to jump,' Sara hiccuped.

'Traditional!' he sputtered. 'Is it traditional to try and drown, too? If you'd tried to go in by the stepping stones first like any normal sane person, you'd have learned that the stones were missing and could have avoided this folly,' he stormed.

Sara shivered. 'Don't yell at me, Brad,' she whispered. 'I'm so cold and still a little scared,' and to her chagrin, hot tears cascaded down her face.

'You deserve to be scared,' he retorted. 'Doing a fool trick like that! How do you think I felt when I went back and saw your white face floating on the water? How would I have explained to your father how I'd gone off and left you here to drown?'

Worry over her father had made him furious, not concern for her, Sara thought dismally. His anger vibrated in the air between them, and she cowered away from him. Her movement drew his attention, and his gaze impassively swept her body, recalling to her mind her current state of undress. With one hand she endeavoured to cover her nakedness, while with the other she fumbled for her clothing, her movements slowed by her chilled limbs. Still maintaining his iron grip on her, Brad grabbed her clothes impatiently and helped her dress, much as if she were a backward child, Sara thought indignantly. Her embarrassing awkwardness at being discovered naked fled in the face of his manifest lack of interest in her body. Sara wasn't certain if she should be angry or grateful. A drowned rat might not be too sexually appealing, but must Brad make the fact of it so readily apparent?

The sun had passed on, and the rock was in the shade now. Sara was thoroughly chilled and could not stop her shivering. Brad muttered a curse and swiftly picked her up and carried her to a clearing in the trees where the sun was expending its last few warm rays. He laid her in a patch of sunlight and then went back to the rock for the remainder of her things.

Sara lay with her eyes closed, drinking in the warmth of the sun. She heard Brad return and place her things beside her. A bug landed on her foot, and she kicked upward.

'Ouch!' Her eyes flew open in surprise.

Brad was rubbing his chin. 'Do you treat all men that way?'

'What do you mean?' Sara asked breathlessly. 'I was shooing away a fly.'

He grinned ruefully. 'That's what I get for trying to be romantic and kiss your foot!'

'Oh,' Sara coloured in confusion. Was Brad playing with her, punishing her in retribution for her frightening him? His swing in mood bewildered her, ranting at her furiously one minute, teasing her affectionately the next. 'What do . . . do . . . you mean?' she managed to stammer.

'Never mind,' he said. 'I ought to be warming your feet, not your heart.' Suiting actions to words, he picked up her white wrinkled foot and briskly rubbed it, causing a sharp, stinging sensation.

Sara tried to jerk her foot away.

'Now what's the matter?' Brad asked.

'It stings.'

'Good,' he said brutally. 'That means the circulation is coming back.' He dropped that foot and began rubbing the second.

Sara bit her lip at the pain, knowing complaining would get her nowhere.

'There,' Brad surveyed her feet in satisfaction. 'Now they're nice and rosy again. Hand me your socks.' He reached out a hand.

Sara pounced on her stockings and held them behind her. 'I'm perfectly capable of putting on my own socks and shoes!' A rage of shivers destroyed any credibility to the sentence, and with a sarcastic look, Brad reached over and grabbed her stockings. She closed her eyes and suffered in silence as he put them on her, but then her feet felt so toasty warm that she couldn't resist wiggling her toes. Crimson, she opened her eyes a slit to see him looking sardonically at her.

'Feels better, I see,' he commented.

'Brad, I . . .' another fit of shivering seized her. She fought it, and then tried again. 'Brad, thank you, I . . .' she shivered again.

'For heaven's sake!' Brad muttered, and swiftly gathered her up in one arm, while with the other he fumbled in his pack. Sara, abstractedly watching him, realised that he must have been fishing all day, as his knapsack held remains of lunch and several beautiful trout. He pulled out a chamois shirt and wrapped it around Sara's shoulders, and then tearing the covering off a chocolate bar, he handed it to her with the command to eat it.

Sara gobbled down the candy, and then the irresistible warmth of Brad's body drew her nearer. Her chilled, numbed limbs refused to respond to her brain's order to move away, and she lay passively in his arms. Soothed by the beat of his heart, she sighed and closed her eyes, exhausted from her struggles in the pool. The sound of his heartbeat mingled with the buzzing of flies and the humming of bees. A lone jay overhead squawked as he flew by. Another fly settled on her lips, and Sara's eyes flew open to see Brad's face bent close to hers.

'It was me again,' he whispered, and his arms tightened.

'Brad?' Sara murmured his name questioningly. Residual shock combined with his unexpected gentleness broke through the barriers she had erected against him. Involuntarily her face raised up, and her lips sought his. Like a soft summer rain, light kisses caressed her mouth, her forehead, her eyelids. Sara fell asleep with the gentle touch of Brad's lips on hers, too tired to puzzle out the meaning of his kisses.

'Sara, Sara,' the voice thrust demandingly into her dreams.

'Go away,' she muttered as she clutched the soft shirt tighter around her.

'Sara, wake up!' the voice insisted.

Sara forced her eyelids open. Brad was looking down at her. Still halfway in her contented dream world, she reached up and kissed his cheek. 'Hello.'

'C'mon, sleepyhead,' he said as he withdrew his arms and forced her to sit up.

'I must have fallen asleep for a few minutes,' she said

guiltily as she noticed Brad flexing his shoulder.

'A few minutes!' he grinned. 'More like two hours!'

'Oh, Brad, I'm sorry,' Sara said in chagrin. 'Why didn't you wake me?'

He lightly flicked her on the cheek. 'It's okay—I only woke you up now because I hear voices on the trail. I think a search party has been sent out.'

'A search party!' She started, and then her face whitened as she saw the huge red ball of a sun was just preparing to dip behind the mountain range. 'Dad must be frantic!' she exclaimed in dismay. 'And your fish,' she remembered. 'Are they spoiled?'

Brad laughed. 'They'll be all right. Get your boots on and see how you feel. I think your rescuers are here,' he added, looking down the trail.

'Dr Livingstone, I presume?' Christy sent the gay query ahead of her.

Josh followed her into the clearing, a frown marring his normally pleasant face. 'What are you doing, Sara? Your dad expected you home hours ago. You really scared him, and he was in quite a state by the time Christy and I arrived home,' he scolded.

Sara hung her head and fixed her eyes on the shoelaces she was attempting to tie.

'A slight mishap,' Brad explained soothingly. 'Nothing that can't be explained.'

'Sara, your hands!' Christy shrieked. 'Did you fall off a mountain?'

Sara hoped she didn't look as embarrassed as she felt. 'No, I didn't fall.' She sent a quick plea for help to Brad, but he was watching the sunset as if he'd never seen one before. 'I, I . . . I cut them trying to climb out of the swimming hole,' she blurted.

'The swimming hole!' Christy looked at her in horror. 'Why, those stepping stones washed away several years ago. There's no way out.'

'Thanks for telling me,' Sara said dryly.

'How did you manage to get out, Sara?' Josh asked curiously.

'Sir Galahad,' Sara airily waved a hand in Brad's direction. 'He came along and rescued the fair maiden.'

'Sara, if you wanted to swim in the pool, you should have told someone—you know Dad's rule. Then you'd have been told about the missing stones,' Christy chided.

'It was an impulse. I was hot and passing by and . . .' Sara's voice trailed off.

'An impulse?' Christy's eyes narrowed. 'I seem to remember your tangerine bathing suit still out on the clothes line.'

Sara could feel her face grow hot and knew she was turning a bright crimson as she devoted herself to tieing her bootlaces.

Suddenly Christy snickered, 'Sara! You were swimming in the nude when Brad rescued you!' At the fierce look from her sister, Christy tried to contain her mirth.

Josh grabbed her arm and propelled her rapidly back down the path. 'Better hurry, you two. It will soon be dark,' he called back over his shoulder. 'We'll go on ahead and reassure the Judge that Sara's okay.' The couple had barely reached the woods before Josh's booming laugh could be heard along with Christy's giggles.

'If you could only see your face!' Brad observed.

'She won't live to be twenty-one,' Sara muttered savagely, standing up and grabbing her pack. Showing only her ramrod-straight back to Brad, she marched off down the trail.

He followed her in silence.

At first Sara hiked rigid with mortification, but halfway home she realised her body was stiff and sore, and her jeans were rubbing away at the raw spots on her knees. She flinched as she blindly stepped into a hole.

Immediately Brad's arm hauled her up by her elbow. 'Here, you're half dead. Give me your knapsack—it weighs a ton. What's in here, anyway?'

'Mostly my camera gear.' Sara gratefully surrendered

her pack. 'Brad,' she drew a deep breath, 'about what happened this afternoon . . .'

'Yes?' His voice was devoid of emotion.

'It doesn't mean anything, just reaction and . . .' Her voice died helplessly away.

'It's okay, Sara. I didn't think it was an invitation to ravage your body. Unfortunately,' he added dryly.

Sara was glad that the growing darkness hid her confusion. Why had Brad said 'unfortunately'? Was he regretting the past, regretting that he had dropped her from his life?

Not once during the past week had he indicated by any word or deed that he thought of Sara as any more than the sister of a friend. If she were honest, she would admit she had wanted, had waited, for Brad to bring up the past, to apologise for his unceremonious dumping of her, to offer an excuse, any excuse for his actions. He had said nothing. Even now, back at the swimming hole, he had viewed her naked body dispassionately with no hint of desire. She had felt that his kisses were offered much as a bandaid would be—comfort, for a sore body. Now she was confused.

What did Brad want from her? What kind of game was he playing with her? He had Ces. Or had he? Perhaps Ces was not as forthcoming as Brad would like. Maybe Brad needed Sara to help him shake up Ces, to make her jealous. The humiliating thought stiffened her spine. Brad would not find it so easy to make use of Sara a second time. He had taught her her lesson too well the first time.

CHAPTER FOUR

SARA could see the Judge pacing anxiously back and forth across the veranda as they drew near. 'Dad, here I am!' she called.

'Sara, my dear!' The Judge hurried down the steps and hugged her tightly to his chest.

'Dad, I'm so sorry that I worried you,' Sara said in a contrite tone.

'You're here now, and fine—that's the main thing. I blame myself for not mentioning the missing stones.' His raised hand forestalled her question. 'Christy and Josh told me about what happened when they arrived back a few minutes ago.'

'Everything?' Sara heard her voice squeak.

Her father was looking past her to Brad and extending his hand. 'There's not adequate words to express my heartfelt thanks, Brad,' he said quietly.

Brad brushed away the thanks. 'It was just luck that I happened along when I did.'

'How did you happen to stumble across the waterhole, Brad?' the Judge asked. 'It's off the marked trail.'

'I heard Sara, so I broke through the underbrush to see what she was up to.'

'You mean you heard her yelling for help?'

'Not exactly. She was . . . well, I guess you could say she was singing.'

'Singing?' The Judge turned a questioning look on Sara.

Sara, recalling that she had been shouting about her virginity to the whole world, and hearing the underlying amusement in Brad's voice, wished the earth would open up and swallow her on the spot. She nodded dumbly in answer to her father's question.

Brad gave her a shove towards the door. 'I think we'd better get Sara inside,' he told her father.

'Of course. I'm sure it's been a horrible experience for you, Sara, and here I am keeping you standing outside talking. Hustle on inside, I'll help Brad in with your things.'

Wearily, Sara started up the back stairs.

'Sara,' Brad's voice stopped her, 'take a nice hot bath and then hop into bed. Someone will bring your dinner up on a tray.'

'Thanks, but I'm not an invalid. The hot bath's a grand idea, but I'll be down for dinner.'

'Sara, I said you'll eat in bed,' Brad repeated with soft menace in his voice. 'I'll be up in thirty minutes and if you're not in bed, I'll tuck you in myself.'

'Really, Brad!' She straightened her tired shoulders and turned to him with snapping eyes. 'Just because you saved my life, don't think you have the right to run it!'

'Thirty minutes,' Brad said sternly.

The Judge chuckled. 'You'd better do as he orders, Sara. Brad is used to having his commands instantly obeyed.'

Brad grinned. 'Your dad is right—I can't have insubordination in the ranks!'

Sara snorted and flounced up the stairs. Deliberately she slammed the door behind her, but felt the gesture lacked in impact when she heard her father and Brad laughing on the other side.

Twenty minutes later, she stepped dripping from the rapidly cooling tub. Ruefully she surveyed her hands and knees which looked as if a vegetable grater had attacked her. Rapidly towelling her hair dry, she thought over Brad's threat to tuck her in. Out loud she said, 'He wouldn't dare!' but an inner voice insisted, yes, he would. Her hands stilled, and she wondered what it would be like to have Brad come and tuck her in, with perhaps a soft goodnight kiss. She remembered his gentle kisses beside the river and the pleasant sensations she had experienced. Perhaps tucking would lead to more passionate kisses, and then . . .

The clicking sound of her bedroom door closing broke into her reverie. Brad already. Hastily she locked the bathroom door. Using her towel, she wiped the moisture from the mirror, and then speedily pulled a comb through the wet tangles of her hair. Thank goodness she'd brought her clothes in with her, she thought. She donned a long-sleeved white nightgown that covered her from ruffled neckline to pink-painted toes peeping beneath bottom ruffles. Small red embroidered flowers scattered about emphasised the innocent and pure look of the nightgown, a look totally belied by the incredible sheerness of the fabric which clearly silhouetted her slim curvy body. From the hook on the back of the door she grabbed her red fleece robe and securely belted it around her waist. She slipped her feet into fuzzy red slippers, took one last look into the mirror, and taking a deep breath to give her courage, unlocked the door and prepared to face Brad.

As she burst through the door like a tornado, the sight of her visitor brought her up short.

'Where's the fire?' Ces was sitting at Sara's dressing table, casually looking at make-up and rummaging through Sara's jewellery box.

'What are you doing here?' Sara demanded.

'Sara, is that all you can ever say to me?' Ces asked in a plaintive voice.

Sara bit her lip. 'I'm sorry, Ces. I was just surprised to see you sitting here.'

'I came to see if you're okay. It's been quite an afternoon, with your father pacing the floor like a caged panther, and then Christy and Josh setting off in a mad search for you. Why, the Judge even suggested I go and look for you!'

Sara giggled at the look of indignation on Ces's face. 'Thanks for checking on me,' she began.

Ces was still intent on listing her grievances. 'And then Josh and Christy come back with some silly story about you almost drowning, and finally Brad gets here and doesn't even apologise for missing our cocktail date which he forgot because of all this ridiculous business of saving you. I finally get him to take one afternoon away from his work, and he wastes it rescuing you!'

Sara couldn't help it. She had to laugh. 'Oh, Ces, I'm sorry Brad thought saving my life more important than a drink with you. If I'd known he had plans when he came by, I'd have weakly waved him on and happily drowned rather than disrupt your date.' Wisely, she didn't refer to the fact that he had also wasted the day fishing somewhere.

Ces reluctantly laughed, too. 'Okay, so it does sound a little selfish when you put it that way, but you are all right, and you did spend the afternoon with Brad while I sat here bored stiff,' she pointed out.

'I didn't exactly spend the afternoon with him.' Remembering the two hours she'd spent sleeping in Brad's arms, Sara nervously picked up her comb and tried to straighten the remaining tangles in her hair. She was aware of Ces's eyes watching her in the mirror, and concentrated harder on her hair.

'What were you swimming in?'

'What?' Sara's arm jerked and caught at a knot, bringing tears to her eyes.

'Your swimsuit is on the clothesline,' Ces stated.

To Sara's immense relief, her bedroom door crashed open, and Christy bounded in.

'Luckily there's no rips or tears in it, but next time I'd appreciate it if you'd ask before you help yourself to my bathing suit, or any of my clothes,' she complained.

'Well, yes, I'm sorry,' Sara said wildly. 'But you were asleep when I left.' Sara realised Christy must have heard Ces's question through the door, and although she herself would tease Sara unmercifully, she rushed to Sara's defence against Ces.

'What is this? A hen party? I told you to be in bed in thirty minutes, Sara.' Brad stood in the open doorway, a mock-stern expression on his face.

'Darling, don't beat her,' Ces jeered. 'Christy and I were just checking on Sara's welfare— right, Sara?'

Sara, whose eyes had immediately flown to Brad at the word 'darling', now looked at Ces. 'Um, yes, thank you for checking up on me.' Darling! Ces called Brad— 'darling', and he certainly didn't seem to mind. Those kisses by the river meant nothing to him. You fool, her mind taunted, those were the kind of kisses Peter would have given you. They were just comfort for a hurt little sister.

'Sara, hop into bed,' Brad's voice ordered summarily.

'I'll go when I'm ready!'

'Are you testing me?' He cocked an eyebrow at her.

'I don't know what you mean.'

'Are you trying to find out if I meant what I said about thirty minutes?'

'Don't be ridiculous. You wouldn't dare!'

Brad openly grinned. 'Now you're daring me.'

'Brad,' Sara stared at the devilish imps in his eyes, her hand clutching the edges of her robe together, 'I'm not daring you to tuck ... to do anything,' she amended quickly. 'As soon as you all leave I'll go to bed.'

Ces frowned at a byplay that excluded her. 'Come on, Christy—I know when I'm not wanted.' She piled Sara's jewellery back into its small silver chest. 'Really, Sara, you shouldn't keep your jewellery all heaped together like this. It will scratch. Well, for heaven's sake! Why are you still lugging this ugly thing around?' She held up a slim metal identification band.

Sara reached out her hand to snatch the bracelet, but Brad was there before her. 'May I?' he asked, and took the bracelet without waiting for Sara's reply. He silently turned the bracelet over and over in his hands for several minutes. Nervously Sara watched his face, but it was wiped clean of any emotion. Deliberately wiped, she felt, as she noticed the clenched jaw.

Finally he spoke. 'I'd heard about these, but this is the first I've seen.' His fingers traced Peter's name inscribed on the P.O.W. bracelet. 'Was this a coincidence, or could you somehow request a certain name?' He glanced at Sara.

'I requested it,' she replied in a stiff voice.

Christy stared wide-eyed at Brad, and even Ces sat motionless as they realised the painful memories Brad must be enduring.

Suddenly Brad became aware of the heavy silence around him. He handed the bracelet back to Ces, who placed it back in the chest and snapped the lid shut.

Not even having been aware she had been holding it, Sara expelled her breath. Now, if only Christy didn't remember. Christy looked at her, and Sara gave her an almost imperceptible negative shake of her head as she saw Christy open her mouth to speak.

Brad's mind was obviously still on the bracelet. 'Peter would have been proud to know you wore this for him, Sara.'

Too emotional to speak, Sara merely nodded.

'Did you two have bracelets, too?' he asked Christy and Ces.

Christy hung her head in shame. 'Yes, but I lost mine after a couple of months.'

'She was only nine,' Sara swiftly defended her sister.

Brad looked questioningly at Ces.

'Certainly not!' she said in a shrill voice. 'It doesn't matter what Sara wears, but I had to consider my image even then. After all, those bracelets are remarkably ugly.'

Sara caught her breath in horror. Did Ces realise what she was saying?

Brad forced a laugh. 'You might have missed a great opportunity there, Ces.'

'How?' Ces was sceptical.

'Well,' Brad drawled, 'there was this girl out in California who was wearing one with the name of one of my buddies on it. It so happened that, unknown to her, he was from the same area. When he was released, the story was in all the local newspapers. She read the article and wrote him a welcome home letter. He was intrigued and looked her up. They're married now with two children.'

'Brad, that's a beautiful story. I think I'm going to cry.' Christy sniffed and ran from the room.

Ces shrugged and stood up from Sara's make-up table. 'And I suppose they'll live happily ever after,' she gibed as she gracefully left the room.

'Yes, I suppose they will,' Brad said thoughtfully. He walked over to the bedroom window, and holding back the curtain, stared out into the black night.

Quietly Sara sat down and finished combing her almost dried hair.

When Brad spoke again, he startled her. 'After Steve got married, he was the buddy in the story,' he explained. 'After Steve got married, I found myself waiting for a letter, too. Oh, I wasn't looking for a wife, but not having any family of my own, I thought it would be nice to know that someone was worried about me, and wore that "ugly" thing.' He snorted. 'A fairy tale, as Ces would say.'

Sara flinched at the note of pain in Brad's voice. She was still a moment, then she resolutely reached for her jewellery chest and opened it. She hadn't wanted Brad to know, but now she dug around until her fingers located the item she wanted. She clenched it in her fist and then turned and crossed the room to his side. In an unsteady voice, she said softly, 'Someone did write you a letter, Brad. You never received it,' and she thrust the object she was holding at his chest.

He took the bracelet, and looked at it in surprise. His thumb rubbed over the indentations forming his name. 'But Peter . . .' he protested.

'I wore two bracelets,' Sara answered.

'You wrote me about this?' Brad persisted.

'That, and several other things.' Her eyes remained downcast. 'I invited you to come visit us,' she added softly.

'Sara, I never got the letter.'

'I know. I didn't have the right address, and it was returned.'

'Sara!' Brad groaned, and then pulled her into his arms.

Realising that he was seeking comfort, Sara encircled his neck with her arms and held him close. For several minutes they stood locked in a quiet embrace.

Brad's voice spoke softly in her ear. 'When we arrived back in the States, I'll never forget what it was like. We got off the plane, and there were hundreds of people waiting—families and loved ones, people hugging and kissing and crying and laughing. I had some buddies waiting to meet me, but it wasn't the same as if someone who loved me and cared about me had been praying for my safe return.' He paused. 'I shouldn't have expected . . . anyone.'

Sara lifted her head from his shoulder. Even years later, the hurt from his empty homecoming was reflected in his eyes. 'Brad,' she said steadily, 'I prayed daily for you. I wrote you a letter every day.'

Agonised, he whispered, 'I never received one.'

She took his head firmly in her two small hands. In a soft but clear voice she spoke. 'I loved you, as I loved Peter.' She had loved him in a different way, but she couldn't tell him that. 'You were loved by someone.'

Brad hugged her closer to him and bending his head, kissed her softly on the lips. 'Thank you for that love, Sara Blanchard,' he whispered.

He lifted his head and stared at her with searching eyes. Then he lowered his head, and his lips fastened once again on hers, only this was no gentle kiss of thanksgiving. He kissed her hard, his lips demanding, seeking.

Sara's lips parted, and she felt her insides dissolve, her legs felt weak, and she clung to him, her hands grasping convulsively his hair. In a daze she felt his hand caress her ear-lobe and slide down the side of her throat. It paused momentarily at her breast, and without thinking she arched her back to thrust her breast into his hand. His fingers slowly cupped its fullness, then she moaned in discontent as the warmth of his hand left her breast and moved slowly, caressingly down her side. She trembled as Brad paused at her waist, then her belt was untied, and he pushed her away to tug back the sides of her robe. He pulled her back into his arms, only this time his arms were inside her robe with only the thin handkerchief fabric of her nightgown between her and Brad's searching hands. Thrills of delight ran on cat feet up and down her spine and delightful unfamiliar warm sensations emanated from her stomach region. She moved closer to Brad and felt her breasts crushed against his hard chest. She was breathing faster now and realised his breathing kept pace. His heart pounded her chest, as his lips once more captivated her mouth. He abandoned her lips, and frustrated, she turned her head into his shoulder, her nostrils revelling in his spicy soap smell mingled with the odour of fresh outdoors along with a slight fishy tang. She squirmed with mounting desire as he feathered kisses on the pulse at her throat and then down to the valley between her breasts. The thin material of her gown offered no impediment as his lips teased her nipples until they thrust firmly out almost as if demanding his lips. Sara looked down at the grey head resting on her bosom. 'Darling,' she thought, bemused, 'Darling?'

Suddenly she realised the 'darling' came from without, not within. She lifted her head, confused.

'Darling?' Ces's voice called from the base of the stairs, 'Brad darling, Sara's tray is ready. Would you please come and get it?'

Slowly Brad held Sara away from him. 'I'll go and get your tray,' he said.

Still befuddled, Sara could only stare at him.

He pulled her robe back together and rested his hands at her waist. 'I'm not your brother. And you're certainly not my little sister!'

Abruptly she pushed him away. Stooping over, she

retrieved her bathrobe tie from the floor and pulled her
robe snugly about her and tied it. She had forgotten
about Ces. If Brad thought that he could play Ces's
lover at night and hers during the day, he had another
think coming! Her face hardened.

'Sara,' Brad reached out for her.

'I thought you said I was supposed to go to bed in
thirty minutes,' she said coldly.

He gave her a quizzical look. 'That doesn't sound like
an invitation for me to join you.'

'Hardly.'

'I thought I was doing pretty good trying to persuade
you to be friends.'

'Friends!' Sara's voice shook with barely suppressed
anger. 'I'd rather be friends with a python! At least when
he smothers you, he has a good reason.'

'I had the impression you were enjoying my
"smothering", as you call it.'

Sara shrugged. 'I must admit you have a very
effective technique.'

'Technique!' Brad exploded. 'That wasn't technique—
that was passion!'

'Brad, I'm really not interested.' That made them
both liars.

His eyes narrowed. 'You seemed pretty interested a
minute ago.'

She clenched her fists and faced him. 'I think you
confuse passion and compassion.'

'Compassion?'

'I felt sorry for you, Brad—such a sob story and all. I
pitied you. I'm sorry if I gave you the wrong
impression.'

Brad stared at her a moment, then turned on his heel.
'I'll bring your dinner up,' he said in an arctic voice.

Sara sank to the bed, surprised her trembling legs had
supported her as long as they had. Realisation hit her
like a cold shower. She had not got over her love for
Brad after all. The love had been merely dormant.
Brad's presence, his smile, his touch, his kisses—all had

combined to act like spring showers on the seeds of love wintering in her heart. Fragile shoots so tiny that she had not recognised them for what they were had sprung up. Love had fully blossomed before she had understood what was happening. How could she have ignored all the signs—her jealousy of Ces, her passionate response to Brad's embrace, the restlessness and discontent she'd felt? Oh, what a fool she had been, to fall in love with Brad all over again! Once again she was in love, and once again Brad thought of her as a pleasant diversion. She had to hide the truth from him.

A knock on the door broke into her tumultuous thoughts, and she braced herself. The five minutes that Brad had been gone had not been sufficient to calm her. 'Come in,' she called in some trepidation. Would he still be angry?

Christy opened the door and walked in balancing a heavily-laden tray on one arm. 'Where do you want me to set this?'

Disappointment and relief warred inside Sara. 'I thought Brad was bringing my tray,' she tried to say casually, but a quiver in her voice betrayed her.

Christy shot her a quick look, but only remarked, 'Apparently Ces had other plans.' She waited until Sara sat up and piled the pillows behind her before lowering the tray to her lap. Then she plopped down in the blue-flowered chaise beside the window.

Sara abstractedly chewed her food. The prime rib tasted like cardboard.

Christy sat gazing pensively out of the window, her chin cupped in her hands. 'There they go now,' she observed.

Sara heard faint sounds of car doors slamming and then an engine roaring to life. She forced herself to take and swallow one more bite before she asked, 'There goes who?'

Christy shot her a scornful glance. 'Brad and Ces, of course. They're going out for dinner.'

'Oh.'

'Oh,' mimicked Christy. 'It seems Brad stood Ces up in order to rescue you, so she told him he owed her a night on the town. I'm hoping Cousin Ces is getting fed up with rural America and wants the bright lights again.'

'Why should you hope that?' asked Sara. 'What has Ces been doing to annoy you?'

'She's such a man-chaser!'

'Don't tell me that after all these years, Josh is succumbing to Ces's fatal charm,' Sara teased.

'No, I don't think I have to worry about Josh, mainly because Ces has no interest in him,' Christy added honestly. 'She seems awfully taken with Brad, however. She's pursuing him pretty hard.'

'Ces isn't interested in a man like Brad. Oh, she admits she's ready to be taken care of and pampered, but before she'll marry and give up her lucrative career, she'll have to find somebody rich. She already has one wealthy beau on her string. Brad is just a summer pastime.'

'Maybe,' conceded Christy. 'But why hasn't she snapped up this wealthy beau, if he's what she's looking for? Besides, Brad is awfully good-looking, even with his scars. As far as money, he did inherit a substantial amount from his parents.'

'Oh.' Sara felt a sinking sensation in the pit of her stomach.

'What's more, Ces and I heard Brad and Dad discussing a talk Brad had had with his publisher. Brad said the publisher thinks this book will be a best-seller, and he's even talking movie rights, paperback and all that stuff. Couldn't that mean millions? The publisher even wants Brad to resign from the service and write full time.'

'What did Brad think about that idea?' Sara asked.

'I don't know,' Christy admitted. 'At that point Ces's eyes lit up, and she started in blabbering to me about what he'd said, and then wanted me to promise I wouldn't let Brad know we'd overheard.'

'Did you promise?'

'I crossed my fingers behind my back when I did,' Christy grinned. 'That day was the beginning of Ces falling all over Brad.'

'I thought she did that from the minute she laid eyes on him,' Sara said dryly.

'Yes, but that was just habit. Now there's a difference. She's like a person with a goal. I haven't said anything to Brad yet, but I might. No matter what Josh says,' she added darkly.

Intrigued, Sara asked, 'What does Josh say?'

'To mind my own business. He said Brad's no fool to be taken up the garden path by a pretty face. Considering what Brad has gone through for his country, I think we owe him a little help in disengaging Ces's tentacles from around his neck.' Christy looked at Sara with speculative eyes. 'For instance, you could save him from Ces.'

'Me?' Sara squeaked.

Christy nodded. 'Why don't you make a play for Brad yourself and save him from Ces?'

'Don't be ridiculous! Brad's a big boy and can certainly rid himself of Ces any time he wants. If he really wants to, that is.'

'Maybe so, maybe not. After all, he is Dad's guest, and Ces is family, so he can hardly be rude to her.'

'Rude?' Sara gave a passable imitation of a laugh. 'If you saw what I saw, rudeness would never enter your mind!' She thought of the night that she had seen Brad and Ces embracing under her window.

'What did you see?'

'Never mind,' Sara said hastily, already sorry that she'd said so much. 'Why are you sitting here anyway? Hadn't you better go and eat?'

'I ate earlier, while you were cleaning up. Josh was in a hurry, and Ces said she and Brad were going out, so Dad, Josh and I ate our meal quickly.' Christy glanced at Sara and then looked away. 'Brad certainly acted surprised when he came downstairs and saw us just finishing up.' Carefully she added, 'I guess Ces hadn't told him yet that they were going out.'

'Christy,' Sara said warningly, 'if you don't quit hinting that Brad is a lamb headed for slaughter, I'll, I'll ... I'll throw this tray at you!'

Christy laughed. 'Better eat your strawberry shortcake first. It's delicious.'

Sara wrinkled her nose at her sister and then obediently picked up her fork and attacked the luscious-looking red and cream-coloured mound.

After Christy had left, Sara put down her fork and began considering her information. It was true that Ces had become more and more paranoid about getting old and losing her looks. She had begun a careful survey of all the men in her wide circle of acquaintances, and one of the first that she had selected as a tentative husband had been Roger Matthews. Wealthy, unmarried, attractive and in his late thirties, Roger had been a prime candidate, but he had dealt with models for years and had immediately recognised Ces's campaign for what it was—a search for security with no love involved. Ces had not been happy when Roger had shown his obvious preference for Sara. She had warned Sara that Roger was a playboy whose only goal was the bedroom. Sara had not had the courage to tell Ces about Roger's marriage proposals, although she knew only Ces's pride was wounded, not her heart.

At present, Ces's brightest prospect was a balding, rotund wealthy businessman in his fifties, named Sam something. He obviously adored Ces, but she continued to put him off. In a rare confiding mood, she had told Sara that she really wanted a man who physically matched her beauty. Sara liked the middle-aged suitor for his many courtesies and his delightful sense of humour and felt terrible about Ces's revelation. But it appeared that Sam was intelligent as well, and once, seeing Sara frown when he appeared with roses and a diamond bracelet, told her that items of great beauty always carried an expensive price tag. Sara was relieved that his love for Ces didn't blind him to her faults, but wondered how two people could be happy in such a limited relationship.

Apparently Ces had come to the Valley with her options still open. At first she had probably viewed Brad as her due entertainment as Christy suggested, but, if Brad turned out to be as wealthy as Christy thought, then Ces would indeed consider him an eligible mate. Sara thought about the past few days and realised that Ces's pursuit of Brad had visibly intensified. If Brad was not working, it was rare to see him without Ces.

Sara giggled inwardly as she remembered that Ces had hauled out yet another of her seemingly inexhaustible supply of needlepoint pillow kits. Ces had once pointed out to Sara that men liked to see a woman sewing because it made her seem more feminine. As a result, Ces was always buying pillow-top kits. She would ostensibly work on it, or have it sitting around in an attractive basket in the living room. After several months she would take the barely started item to the nearby yarn shop, where, for an exorbitant fee, the proprietress would obligingly finish the piece and construct the pillow. The first time the latest boy-friend had seen the finished pillow he had been struck with amazement and had copiously complimented Ces on her talent and her beauty—compliments that Ces had graciously received as her due. Hearing this byplay for the first time, Sara had waited for Ces to explain about Mrs Neal at the yarn store. When Ces remained quiet, Sara had begun to blurt out the facts, whereupon Ces had looked at her with a fixed stare that definitely said 'shut up'. Later Sara had protested that Ces was less than honest.

Ces had only shrugged. 'It makes the man happy to see what a homebody I am, I'm happy because I have a new pillow, and Mrs Neal's happy to get the money. Surely you wouldn't deny us all that happiness, Sara?' Ces asked in a wheedling tone.

Sara suspected that Ces was mocking her, but she had maintained a straight face and replied that of course, Ces was right to keep everyone happy. After that Sara had managed with great equanimity to listen to all the compliments on Ces's cleverness and skill from her various escorts, and had come to equate the hauling out of the sewing basket with the appearance of a new male target on the scene.

In the past Sara had never cared enough about Ces's escorts to expose her little deceptions. She contemplated pointing them out to Brad, but shrugged away the temptation. Brad was a big boy. If he preferred frivolous, feminine and devious women, what did she care?

CHAPTER FIVE

SARA sat idly rocking on the veranda. She was watching with amusement the antics of the animals and birds at the feeder. A chickaree, one of the mountain's tiniest squirrels, was selfishly chasing away all the birds, and confiscating the largest and most delectable morsels from the feeder. He ran down the tree the feeder was nailed to, then scurried fifty feet to another large pine tree. Swiftly he scaled his way to the topmost branches and secreted his hunk of cake there next to the trunk. Then the squirrel turned and rapidly made his way back to the feeder. Meanwhile, a grey jay was perched on the electric wires watching the scene with bright, alert eyes. As soon as the chickaree touched the ground again, with a loud squawk, the jay swooped over to the pine tree, grabbed the food and triumphantly flew away. The chickaree never even looked up. Delightedly Sara laughed at the brazen jay as the scene was enacted time and time again while she watched.

'Those jays are clever little devils, aren't they?' Sara's father was grinning as he sat down beside her.

Sara smiled in agreement.

'It's been several days since your horrible experience. How are you feeling?'

'Lovely!' Sara breathed deeply. 'I think I could be content here for ever.'

'That's good to hear, Sara. I was worried that coming here this first time would be very upsetting to you. So many memories . . .'

'At first it was,' she admitted. 'But, Dad, how can anyone sit in the midst of all this peace and beauty and not feel some contentment? The blue skies, the mountains, the flowers, the animals . . .' Sara gestured helplessly. 'There's no way to describe it, but I'm just moved by all this loveliness. It erases mean thoughts, makes me want to embrace the world, be kind to everyone . . .' she paused. 'I suppose that sounds rather silly.'

'Not at all, Sara. You have always had an infinite capacity to absorb beauty, and with so much beauty here, I can imagine you're filled with it. In fact, it almost seems to me, you reflect this beauty and glow from within.'

'Why, Dad, what a lovely compliment!' Sara arose and bent over to kiss her father on the cheek. 'You wouldn't be angling for a favour?' she teased, trying to cover her embarrassment and the warm enjoyment caused by her father's words.

Her father turned to look at her as she once again curled up in her wicker chair. 'As a matter of fact . . .' he hesitated.

Sara laughed. 'I do believe you're afraid to ask! You know I'd do anything for you.'

'Well, the fact is, Sara, it's a favour for me and yet not for me. It seems that in Vietnam, Peter and Brad used to talk about the lake, and now Brad has a strong desire to go up there and camp out for a week or so.'

'What has that got to do with me?'

'I don't want to let him go up there alone. I'd prefer at least two people. That's primitive country up there, and if anything should happen to Brad . . .' the Judge's voice trailed off.

'Send Josh,' Sara said promptly.

'I asked Josh, but he can't get off.'

'Then I guess Brad will just have to skip the lake.'

'You could always go with Brad,' he suggested. 'Just for a week.'

'No,' Sara said instantly.

Her father frowned at the implacable note in her voice. 'I don't ask many favours of you, Sara . . .'

'Please, Dad,' Sara interjected hurriedly, 'don't ask me this one. It's not so important that Brad go, is it?' She pleaded with her father to agree.

'I've benefited so much from Brad's friendship,' her father demurred, 'I hate to reject the one favour he's asked of me.' The Judge sighed. 'I suppose I could go. If I take it real slow, this old thing should be okay.' He made a pathetic gesture in the direction of his heart.

'Dad, you wouldn't!' Sara cried, aghast.

He shrugged. 'You leave me little choice, Sara. I'm sure I could manage.'

'You mean you don't leave me much choice, don't you?' she asked bitterly.

'You mean you'll go up with Brad?'

Sara eyed her father dryly. 'Was there ever any doubt in your mind?'

Her father tried to keep a straight face, but failed. 'No doubt at all,' he agreed. 'You're too nice a person to let me down, Sara,' he added sincerely.

'Flattery gets you everywhere,' she mocked. 'Does Brad know the treat in store for him?'

'I told him I'd prefer two people went instead of him trekking up there alone. I explained that Josh and I were unable to go, but that I'd put the question to you.'

'What was his reaction to that?' Sara asked in a carefully schooled voice.

'Brad said that would be fine with him. Why wouldn't he be happy to have you as a guide? You spent almost as much time at the lake as Peter did.'

'How can Brad leave his book?' And silently Sara added, how can he leave Ces?

'He said he's done except for a couple of spots that aren't quite right. He's probably been working too hard. A few days away will give him a fresh perspective.'

Her father rose and crossed behind her chair. He gripped her shoulder hard in passing. 'Thanks, Sara. I appreciate what you're doing more than I can say.'

Quick tears sprang to her eyes, and she nodded weakly in acknowledgment as her father went indoors.

'Oh no,' she moaned to herself, 'I can't, I can't!' How could she possibly survive a situation as fraught with emotional pitfalls as this camping trip would entail? To spend a week in such close proximity with Brad was asking more than any human could possibly endure. If only she had fallen down the stairs her first night here and broken her leg! There was no way she could carry off her pretence of friendship with Brad for a solid week in a setting as romantic and intimate as the lake. She'd have to tell her father no, she couldn't do it. Halfway to her feet, she stopped. She couldn't back out now. Her father may have been lightheartedly threatening to take Brad himself, but on the other hand, it was exactly what he would do if she refused to go. It was emotional blackmail, but Sara knew she was trapped into complying with her father's request. She slumped back into her chair, self-pity engulfing her in waves.

Conversation at the dinner table that evening was exploded by the topic of the camping trip. It was the Judge who casually announced that Sara and Brad were leaving in the morning to camp out at the lake for a week.

Ces was outraged. 'Camping? You're going up to the lake for a whole week, alone, just you and Brad?'

Sara could have cheerfully strangled her. 'Actually, I haven't had a chance to talk to her, but I thought that maybe Christy might like to go along.' She sent a wordless plea to her sister.

Christy ignored the cry for help. 'Not me. Brad just wants to spend the whole week mooning over some trout, and fish never were my favourite conversationalists.'

'Thanks!' Sara hissed at her sister.

Like a dog with a bone, Ces could not let the subject go. 'It doesn't seem quite right, just the two of you in that isolated spot . . .'

Sara seethed, but before she could answer Ces, the Judge cut in. 'It was my idea, Ces. Brad wanted to see the lake, and as his host, I wanted to fulfil his wish, if possible. Sara is the only person available who's qualified to guide Brad up there. Surely you don't think

I'd let them do something that's—well, shall we say, unsuitable?'

Ces's dilemma rendered her silent. To go on would be to accuse Sara's father of poor judgment. Momentarily she sought refuge in a pout.

Brad quickly jumped into the breech with a question about the fishing at the lake. Josh and Christy followed his lead and steered the conversation into less controversial channels. Sara sat quietly, sliding the food aimlessly around her plate, resenting the position into which Brad and her father had placed her.

'I believe I'll go along with Brad and Sara,' Ces's honeyed tones shattered the hum of conversation.

'Go along?' Sara looked at her father in horror. Ces was a pain on a camping trip as she hated every aspect of 'roughing it', and consequently made all around her miserable. Sara opened her mouth, but her father forestalled her negative retort.

'Certainly not, Ces! I wouldn't think of it. It's extremely kind of you to offer, but I know what a sacrifice you would be making, and I can't allow you to do that. Besides, I haven't been able to spend much time with you this trip, an omission we can remedy while Brad and Sara are grubbing up at the lake.'

Stymied in her efforts, Ces could only graciously agree with the Judge. She devoted the remainder of the meal to acting the part of the abandoned waif, until to Sara's disgust, Brad attempted to appease her by asking her to go out for a drink that evening.

After dinner, Sara was waiting on the veranda stairs when Brad came back to fetch Ces. Perhaps she could persuade him not to go. She was trying to decide how to phrase the request when Brad spoke first.

'I've been dreaming about that lake for years now, Sara. I can't tell you how much I appreciate your volunteering to take me up. When the Judge told me he preferred that I shouldn't go alone and suggested you would guide me, I was positive you'd refuse.'

Sara started to deny she had ever done anything so

foolish as to volunteer to accompany Brad anywhere, but at that moment her father strolled out on the veranda, and the opportunity was lost.

The Judge seemed to sense Sara's tension, and he asked quickly, 'Am I interrupting anything?' while at the same time he shot a stern look at Sara, as if he could read her thoughts.

Brad hastened to assure him that they were merely discussing their forthcoming trip, then he enthused about the anticipated pleasures of the fishing. Numb, Sara let the flow of words wash over her. The clicking of high heels announced Ces's entrance. After a few comments on the fine evening, she and Brad disappeared into the night.

Sara's father sat down on the steps beside her. 'Courage fleeing?' he asked gently. She nodded, and his arm encircled her shoulders. 'If I didn't feel an obligation——' he began.

'I understand,' Sara interrupted.

'Blast this heart of mine!' he exploded. 'I've a good mind to ignore doctor's orders and go anyway.'

'Don't be silly,' she chided him. 'I'll be fine. I was nervous about coming to the valley, and that's been okay. This trip will work out. It's just that . . .' her voice trailed away.

'I know, I know. More memories of Peter.' Her father sighed deeply. 'I haven't forgotten the many times you and Peter camped at the lake.'

Sara was thankful for the cooling night breezes fanning her flushed face. Her father thought Peter was the cause of her reluctance. She couldn't tell him that she feared her own susceptibility to Brad's charms.

'I trust Brad, you know.' Unexpectedly her father's words ran in the same vein as her thoughts. 'You don't—well, you don't have to—er—worry about him,' her father added awkwardly.

Sara blanched. What would her father think if she asked, did he trust her? She answered her own question. He'd think she was crazy.

Slowly her father hoisted himself upright. 'Better get to bed, Sara,' he advised. 'Brad wants an early start in the morning.'

'He's not in bed,' Sara argued childishly.

Her father chuckled. 'True, but what would he say if I started bossing him around? Come on.' He held out his hand and helped her to her feet, and together they went inside.

As the first streaks of dawn appeared on the horizon, Sara found herself seated in the heavily laden four-wheel-drive vehicle and heading back into the Valley towards the pass at the far end. She stole a glance at Brad seated beside her casually attached to the wheel. In his tight jeans, blue plaid wool shirt and brown laced boots, he exuded sensuous masculinity. Sara resented his alert air when he'd been out half the night. She had lain awake for hours but had never heard Ces come in, and now she felt woozy from lack of sleep. As if he sensed her appraisal, Brad turned and smiled at her, his white teeth glinting in the morning's half light. Trying to ignore the rioting sensations in her stomach, Sara gave a fleeting smile back.

'Warm enough?' Brad enquired. 'This morning air is nippy even in the middle of the summer.'

'I'm fine. I'm very bundled up.' She indicated her red ski sweater pulled on over a white cotton shirt and jeans. Heavy wool socks peeped over the tops of sturdy hiking boots.

Brad nodded in acknowledgment, and they drove on in silence.

Driving demanded all Brad's concentration, and Sara was glad of a chance to marshal her forces. The trail was a torturous, twisting ribbon, at times disintegrating into two faint ruts. They bumped and bounced their way ever upward out of the Valley with only a short stop to consume the lunch packed by Mrs Collins. Sara's eyes strayed several times to the altimeter attached to the dashboard, and each time she marvelled at their steep climb. At one point, their progress was slowed to a mere crawl when they ascended into the white nothingness of a morning cloud still lingering down below the peaks. When they pulled out of the cloud-induced fog, Sara caught her breath in delight at the panorama spread below her. They had scaled a minor pass, and another valley much like their own spread beneath them. Brad rolled the car to a stop, and without speaking, they each jumped out of the vehicle and walked to the edge of the track where they gazed silently around them.

Far below a small blue jewel nestled deep in the valley and glistened in the morning sun. Immediately before them, the land sloped sharply down hill and ran riotous with the summer wildflowers. Clumps of yellow biscuit-root and pink sticky geraniums ran side by side with mountain bluebells and scarlet Indian paintbrush, while interspersed here and there were blue columbine and the ubiquitous dandelion. A tinkling sound to Sara's right drew her attention, and she almost crooned at the lovely sight of the effervescent water leaping and jumping from stone to stone as it made its merry way to the lake far below. On both sides of the stream white globe flowers pushed up through heavy green carpets of their leaves. A movement above her caught her eyes, and shading them from the intense sun, she looked up to see a Golden Eagle soaring majestically overhead. He flew to a far peak, and fascinated, her eyes followed him, only to be distracted by the beauty of the surrounding peaks. Above the timberline, the peaks were granite blue in the afternoon sun, with here and there pinkish patches of unmelted snow. Sara made no move to fetch her camera. No lens could capture this moment for her, but it would be for ever etched in her memories.

Lost in contemplation of the grandeur before her, she gradually became aware that Brad was speaking to her. She glanced at him and realised that at some point he must have returned to the car, because he was now using binoculars to scan the valley below.

'Did you say something?' she queried.

'I was just thinking out loud. No wonder Peter's thoughts constantly returned to this place when we were back in that hellhole. This is everything that wasn't— clean, pure, almost holy. You feel that no evil has ever occurred here.' He uttered a short laugh, lowered his binoculars and turned to look at Sara. 'That probably sounds ridiculous to you. Romanticising a place, giving an inanimate place human qualities.'

She answered him softly. 'No, I don't think it's ridiculous. I've often felt this place had a cleansing effect on me. It's impossible to hate up here. In fact,' she giggled, 'this was Dad's secret weapon to fight sibling brawling.'

'What do you mean?'

'Whenever Peter and I were going at it tooth and nail, and we did frequently, as much as we loved each other.' She paused. 'It's funny,' she said quietly, almost as if talking to herself, 'until this moment, for years I'd forgotten that Peter and I ever had a cross word with each other. I only remembered the good times, the kind words . . .' Her voice trailed off as the destructiveness of her grief struck her with appalling clarity. She had always looked up to Peter and adored him, but since his death she had gone beyond that. She had put him up on a pedestal so high that she had dehumanised him. Only since returning to the valley was she remembering the loving and vital person that her brother had been. Perhaps the greater tragedy was not Peter's death, but the damage she had done to his memory. Her mind was tentatively groping its way to this new understanding when she suddenly recalled Brad's presence. Quickly she brushed the back of her hand across her wet lashes and cleared her throat. 'Anyway,' she said in a stronger voice, 'when Peter and I were really fighting hard, and I suppose driving Dad to distraction, he would send the two of us up here camping. All the way up the trail we would yell horrid, nasty things at each other. Once, about half a mile from the top, Peter made such a snide remark, I forget what it was, but I was so mad I slugged him in the arm. It's a wonder we didn't go off the trail over the side! Peter was so furious he shoved me out of the car and drove off and left me to trudge up the remainder of the way. I occupied my mind while climbing up the road devising novel ideas for his approaching homicide! When I reached the top, hot, dirty, seething and filled with revenge, the car sat here, but no Peter. That made me even more furious to have my plans thwarted. After I'd sat here twenty minutes or so, all the mad just oozed away like mud through a crack. Peter must have been watching my face, because he then emerged from behind a huge boulder where he'd been hiding, hand outstretched to shake.'

'So you were friends again, and you never needed your revenge.'

Sara coloured softly and couldn't meet Brad's eyes. 'I forgave Peter, but I didn't forget,' she muttered.

'What did you do?'

'I jumped in the car, and as Peter had left the keys in the ignition, I just drove off and left him to walk down.'

Brad slapped his thigh and roared with laughter. Sara joined in, her voice blending with Brad's deep laugh.

He finally wiped his streaming eyes. 'I'm surprised you're still alive today!' he managed to gasp.

Sara grinned, shamefaced. 'Well, he was pretty livid, but he had to admit fair is fair. Besides,' she added, 'I'd walked uphill while he only walked downhill, and when he arrived at camp, I'd already done all the work, the camp was set up, and even a glass of cold water awaited him.' She giggled. 'I'll never forget the look on his face when he arrived in camp! For a minute I thought I'd finally gone too far. I wasn't even supposed to be driving yet, because I was too young.'

'What then?' Brad prompted.

'The magic of the setting went to work on us, and we became best buddies again and had a wonderful time.' She grimaced. 'The whole family camped up here frequently, but Peter and I never called the lake by its proper name. To us it was always Reconciliation Lake.'

'Reconciliation Lake,' Brad mused. 'Do you suppose your dad knew you called the lake that?'

'Don't be silly! He just sent us up here to get us out of his hair until we'd fought out what was bothering us.' She turned and headed back to their vehicle.

'Hmmm.' Brad was pensive as he climbed in behind the wheel and started up the engine.

As they began their descent, Sara's mind was racing. Surely her father had no ulterior motives in sending her and Brad up here? She examined all her actions of the past week. Was it possible that her father realised her love for Brad, and thought that close proximity might resurrect old dreams? Maybe all along he knew about Reconciliation Lake and had deliberately sent her and Brad up here to let the lake work its magic on them. Now she recalled her father's gentle but adamant dissuasion of Ces when she had suggested that she accompany them. At the time Sara had been merely thankful that she wouldn't have to cope with Ces. She had thought that her father was merely thinking of Ces. Now she wondered. She put cool hands to hot cheeks. She had talked too much. If Brad suspected her father's motives . . . She stole a glance at him. As if sensing her look, he turned and grinned at her, a diabolical imp dancing in his eyes. Quickly Sara looked out of the window. Brad was amused at the situation. He had reached the same conclusion as she, but he had leapt to it, while she was meandering around in the past. Now it was up to her to convince Brad that her father had no foundation for his scheming. She forced a laugh that sounded false even to her ears. 'Poor Dad—such a romantic! I suspect he thinks we'd make a good match, and this is his way of promoting it.'

A particularly deep pothole claimed Brad's attention. Finally he spoke. 'He probably doesn't realise that you and I don't like each other much.' He sent a quick apologetic glance at Sara. 'You're just not my type.'

To her horror, Sara heard her voice quaver, 'Just what exactly is your type?'

'A warm loving armful,' Brad replied quickly.

'Like Ces, I suppose,' Sara sniffed disdainfully.

'I'm not sure I'd classify Ces as a warm and loving armful,' he said doubtfully.

'You've done enough research, you ought to know,' she retorted.

'Now what's that supposed to mean?'

'Nothing.' Sara silently cursed herself for hinting that she had seen any of their embraces.

'Spying?' asked Brad, amused.

'Certainly not!'

'You seem pretty certain Ces has been in my arms.'

'If a person insists on kissing another person in the back porch light right under my window, I can hardly help it if I see them!'

Sara felt Brad glance at her, but he said nothing and in a few moments he began whistling tunelessly through his teeth. She forced herself to look out at the view.

Presently Brad spoke again. 'Sara, I know a reconciliation is out of the question for us, but do you suppose that just for this week we could forget the past? Could we declare a truce and be friends?'

For a moment anger made Sara see fiery red pinwheels. That Brad could even consider forgetting the past showed all to clearly how unimportant she had been to him. Then common sense asserted itself, and she knew his suggestion was the only practical way for her to endure the week's stay at the lake. She answered Brad steadily, 'Yes, I'd like that. A truce it is,' she affirmed. His approving nod warmed her.

When at last they had descended to the lake, Sara felt battered and bruised. The past winters with their abundant snowfalls and the resulting torrential spring run-offs had washed out large sections of the track. In other areas, huge boulders had become loose from their resting places in the mountainside and had tumbled down to rest in the middle of the road, often with an accompanying rock slide which blocked off large sections of the road. More than once Sara had held her breath in sheer terror as Brad had flung the wheel sharply to avoid a hazard and their left side wheels had seemed to hang out in space. When Brad had at last reached the trail's end, he had switched off the engine and sat with his hands clutched, white-knuckled, on the wheel.

'An exciting ride,' Sara said with a shaky laugh. 'I hope I recover in time to brave it for the trip back out!' She opened the car door and stepped out, only to grab the door as her legs, stiff from pressing the floorboards, momentarily buckled.

Brad turned to look at her. 'You okay?'

'A little stiff,' she admitted. 'That was a wild ride.'

Brad nodded. 'I think that road is one of the worst I've ever driven. Do you mean to tell me that you and Peter drove that all the time as teenagers?'

'It's never been that bad before. The recent weather extremes have taken their toll. Also, no one in the family has come this way lately, so Dad didn't know what it was like.'

'Next time I come by mule!'

Sara laughed in agreement.

As if my mutual consent, they began unloading the vehicle and preparing to set up camp. 'I'll check the stores and you can put up the tents. Okay?' Sara asked.

'No "S"—tent, as in one,' said Brad, hauling out a large canvas bundle and setting it on the ground.

She gave a quick frown. 'I don't understand.'

'Your dad said the other tent, the small one, had long ago rotted and been discarded. We can flip a coin to see who gets this one, or,' seeing her outraged face, he added generously, 'you take the tent, and I'll sleep outside on the ground.'

Sara hesitated, and finally said firmly, 'No, Brad, that's silly. This tent is our old family tent, and it's huge. You sleep on one side, and I'll take the other side.'

He looked at her steadily a moment. 'You're sure you don't mind?'

'Certainly not,' Sara answered coolly. 'I trust you to remain on your own side of the tent.'

'What will the neighbours think?' Brad gestured around them at the primitive wilderness.

She laughed. 'You could sneak in after dark and be on your way by dawn,' she suggested mischievously.

He laughed too, then picked up the canvas bag with the tent equipment and walked away.

Sara busied herself with the cooking stores trying to decide where best to set up the kitchen. Behind her she could hear the ringing tones of the sledge on the tent stakes. Finally there was silence and Sara turned to look at the tent. She bit her lip in dismay as Brad walked over to the car.

He tossed two sleeping bags up on his shoulder and then disappeared into the tent. 'Which side do you want?' his muffled voice called out.

'The uphill side,' Sara replied.

Brad's face appeared in the tent opening. 'What do you mean, uphill side?'

Without answering, she picked up a cup and filled it with water. Walking over to the tent's nearest corner, she emptied the water out on to the ground. The little river that formed immediately ran downhill the length of the tent.

Brad's face disappeared back into the tent, and Sara could hear muttered curses and see the canvas sides of the tent shaking. Brad's boots appeared, followed by his kneeling form as he backed out of the tent, once again shouldering two sleeping bags.

She started to laugh, but after a quick glance at his face, she swallowed her laugh and hurried to take a sleeping bag from him.

In total silence the poles were taken down from the tent, and the canvas collapsed. Then the only sound was that of the crowbar shoving the stakes out of the ground.

Ostentatiously polite, Brad turned to Sara and asked, 'Where do you want the tent?'

Silently Sara pointed to a level area farther back from the lake and nearer the trees. She cleared the area of the few sticks and rocks, then helped Brad haul the tarpaulin into the centre of the cleared area. Taking a corner of the tent, she helped him settle it on the tarpaulin. With a resigned air, Brad took up the heavy sledge, and once again the loud ringing of metal against metal pealed as he pounded in the heavy tent stakes. Sara gathered up the light aluminium tent poles, she and Brad placed them in the centre socket and with a heave the tent was up, and the poles were firmly wedged in the ground.

Brad stalked over to the sleeping bags heaped on the ground. Once again flinging them to his shoulders, he disappeared into the tent. His face reappeared. 'Which side?' he asked through clenched teeth. 'And if you dare to let that lurking laughter out, I'll strangle you!'

That did it. Sara sank to the ground and burst into helpless laughter. 'It doesn't ... doesn't ... matter ... matter which side,' she stuttered as she struggled for control.

Brad grinned wryly. 'I never was a Boy Scout,' he confessed as he went back into the tent.

Sara set up the aluminium picnic table, snapping its flimsy-looking legs securely into place. At one end she placed the bottled gas stove. Her eyes smiled as she hummed to herself. Maybe this trip would be good fun after all. Brad was proving to be an agreeable companion, and there was no reason why she couldn't enjoy this little jaunt with him. It would be no different from camping with Peter or Josh, she assured herself.

'Need a hand here?' Brad's voice came from over her shoulder.

Startled, she leaned back against him, her hands crossed below her throat. 'You surprised me.'

His hands settled lightly on her shoulders. 'You must have a guilty conscience to jump like that.'

'Don't be silly,' Sara smiled. Inside her whole being was still wildly jumping at the close contact with Brad.

Her shoulders seemed to throb where his hands rested, and she knew she should move away, but she seemed rooted to the spot. She wanted his arms around her. She wanted his kisses. In spite of his scars and grey hair, Brad was one of the most attractive men she knew. She couldn't let him know that she had fallen in love with him. Determined to remain calm, she willed herself to walk away from him to the car.

'You can carry that wooden box over there. Be careful, it's heavy,' she warned.

Brad staggered under the weight. 'What's in here anyway, a ton of bricks?'

'It's the camp kitchen with all our cooking supplies and utensils. See?' She opened a catch, and the front of the box dropped open to reveal a compartmented interior stuffed with pans, plates, condiments and all the other essentials of a camping trip.

Brad whistled. 'Pretty impressive! I can't believe you've forgotten anything.'

'I shouldn't have. Dad built this box years ago, and after each trip it's repacked and all ready to go again. This list here,' she pointed to a piece of paper taped inside the lid, 'is a reminder of what belongs in the box.'

'A clever idea.' Brad poked about in the contents of the box.

'Born of necessity,' she explained. 'Our first camping trip Dad forgot the matches. Luckily Mom still smoked and had her cigarette lighter. Unfortunately, she hadn't brought extra fluid for it, so of necessity, its use was rationed. Mom had to cut way down on her smoking and was vyr disagreeable the entire trip, snapping at us all. Later it became a family joke, but it wasn't very funny then.'

'So your dad built the box.'

'No, not then,' Sara admitted. 'The next trip, Dad remembered the matches, but Mom forgot the salt. That time we spent the whole trip snapping at her! One week after our return she handed Dad a set of drawings and told him she wouldn't set foot on another camping trip until he'd built her a camp kitchen.' Sara laughed. 'After that our camping trips were much more enjoyable.'

'I can see that they would be.'

By now they had totally set up their camp. The tent was firmly anchored on solid level ground and ideally located near a large tree, not too close in case of lightning, but close enough in case of a rare marauding bear. In the centre of the clearing Brad had built a fire ring, using the fire-blackened stones from past campfires and locating it in the old charred area. Lumber from home was stacked by the fire ring. Nearby two plastic woven aluminium lawn chairs had been set up. A safe distance from the fire ring sat the kitchen, which consisted of the picnic table with the camp kitchen, the gas stove and a five-gallon water container with a spigot. A solar water bag had been filled and hung on the southern branches of a pine tree where the sun's rays could heat it for bathing. The coolers and boxes of food remained in the car where they were convenient to reach but safe from inquisitive animals.

Sara looked around in satisfaction. 'There's no place like home.'

Brad smilingly agreed. 'We should be able to manage nicely here. Anything else need to be done?'

'That should be it. Unless you want to toss for who cooks dinner?'

Brad looked with longing at the nearby lake, and Sara could see that he was itching to fetch his fishing gear and try out the waters. She took pity on him. 'Tell you what—why don't you go try for some fish for dinner, and I'll see what else we have here to go with them.'

'You're a trump, Sara!' He gave her a quick hug, grabbed his fishing tackle and jogged towards the lake. 'I won't be long,' he shouted over his shoulder.

'I'll bet,' Sara muttered. She wandered aimlessly around the camp for a few minutes, admittedly a little cross at being deserted for a fishing pole. That ought to convince her if nothing else did that Brad considered her a friend and nothing else. She couldn't see him abandoning Ces for some silly old trout. She glanced at her watch and decided she didn't need to start any preparations for dinner for a couple of hours. She looked disconsolately about the camp, but nothing there needed done. Finally she grabbed up her camera equipment and headed up the slopes away from the lake.

The sun was heading towards the west, casting interesting shadows where the few trees in this area raised their windswept arms to the sky. Sara busied herself capturing the personality of these hardy specimens which defied nature and eked out their own kind of existence. Each tree portrayed its own dominant personality, and Sara admired their bizarre beauty. Climbing ever higher, she crowed with delight when she discovered a wild rose thrusting its gentle blossoms up beside one of the grotesque trees, the delicate pinks and greens of the flower contrasting sharply with the gnarled grey wood. Occasionally she interrupted her picture-taking to glance down to the lake to see if Brad was having any success. If he was, Sara hadn't seen it. She was trying to immobilise one bloom of the rose plant when she realised that the wind was rising. Where she was standing, an outcropping of rock provided a slight windbreak, but down by the lake, small white caps were beginning to form. Brad was hunched down into his shirt collar, but showed no signs of giving up. Sara gathered her gear together and hurried downhill to the camp.

The sun began to set, turning the sky into a child's painting with huge splashes of red, peach and magenta searing across the blue background. With the sun going down, the air was becoming chill, and Sara quickly threw on her sweater. Rummaging through the contents of the large styrofoam freezer, she found several hamburgers and placing them in a skillet, put them on to fry. An open can of beans, minus the paper label, went on next, followed by potatoes sliced into the skillet. When everything was seasoned to Sara's taste, and cooking satisfactorily, she turned her attention to the fire ring. She crumbled up several newspapers followed by a handful of wood shavings and some small twigs. Balanced carefully on top, she placed two pine logs. Striking a match, she applied it to the newspaper and sat back triumphantly on her heels as the shavings and then the twigs quickly blazed. It would be only a few minutes before the logs ignited too.

She heard stones rattling and turned to see Brad coming up the trail wearing a chagrined expression and carrying rod and tackle box, but no fish. He stepped into the clearing and sniffed suspiciously at the smell of dinner cooking. Quickly he went over to the stove and peered into the skillet. 'It seems you don't have a lot of faith in my fishing abilities,' he accused.

Sara wasn't about to admit that she'd been watching him. 'I saw the wind on the lake. One seldom catches fish when it's windy.'

Brad was breaking down his rod and stopped to look at her in surprise. 'Do you fish?'

'I used to.'

'Why not any more?'

'I'd reached the point where I spent more time taking pictures than fishing, and it wasn't worth the money to buy me a fishing licence. However, both Dad and Peter were avid fishermen, and they argued lures, methods, fishing secrets and the like for hours on end. In spite of ourselves, Christy and I are practically experts on the subject. Even Ces knows more than the average person, just through her summer vacation exposure.'

'I must admit I have trouble visualising Ces out fishing,' he commented.

'She does occasionally.' Honesty compelled Sara to defend her cousin.

Sara marvelled at how easily she and Brad slipped into an easy companionship. They laughed and chatted their way through supper. Brad told amusing incidents about his friends and work, and she countered with inside stories about advertising foibles. Together they cleaned up the few dishes and then chatted as they later sat by the fire.

The campfire was beginning to die down now, and the night air was chill. Sara hugged her body close with her arms, glancing over at Brad sitting in the lounge chair across the fire. They had been sitting quietly in a comfortable silence for some moments. As much as Sara hated to break up the friendly atmosphere, she could feel her eyelids becoming leaden. She looked up at the sky. 'The stars always seem so much brighter, so much closer, out here,' she murmured half to herself, half to Brad. The heavily star-studded sky reminded her of a visit to a planetarium where the ceiling had blazed with pinpricks of light representing the various stars and constellations.

Brad followed her gaze upward. 'Beautiful—look! There's the Big Dipper.' He pointed to the familiar constellation.

Sara gazed into the sky for several moments and then stood up and stretched. 'I think I'll go to bed now. I want to catch the sunrise.' She stood for a few seconds, then asked awkwardly, 'Do you want me to get ready for bed first, or I can wait out here . . .' her voice trailed off.

Matter-of-factly, Brad ignored her confusion. 'You go ahead. I think I'll stay out here and enjoy the stars a little longer.'

'Well, goodnight, then.' Sara was thankful he hadn't commented on her obvious embarrassment. Of course sleeping in a tent with her didn't bother him. She was just someone's sister. He even said that she wasn't his type. Stifling a sigh, Sara went into the tent and quickly pulled off her jeans and shirt. She thought she heard Brad ask a question and called, 'What?' but there was no answer. She knelt down and in the pitch dark of the tent fumbled in her bag until her fingers recognised the texture of her nightwear. Shivering a little in the cold, she pulled off her underwear, then thrust one foot and then the other into her nightclothes and swiftly pulled it up over her shoulder. She was just buttoning up the last button at the top when the tent flap was pulled back.

'I said wait a second, and I'll light the lantern for you,' Brad said as he entered the tent carrying the lantern.

Startled, Sara turned to look at him. He stood, open-mouthed, staring at her, then a broad grin appeared on his face. Carefully he set down the lantern, and putting his hands on his hips, surveyed her from head to toe before bursting out laughing. 'What in the world are you wearing?'

Sara laughed, and then assumed a pose she'd seen models demonstrate many times. One hand on hip, the other gracefully flung to one side, she minced forward and professionally turned to one side and then the other, all the while reciting in a cool detached tone, 'Before you, you see Madam Sara's latest creation—nightwear for camping. Note the exquisite lines of the drop seat for midnight forays and the waffle weave for warmth. The style of the long sleeves and buttoned-up front lend an air of innocence denied by the passionate red of the fabric and the body-hugging lines of this union suit ...'

Brad's eyes narrowed. 'Are you being deliberately provocative, Sara?'

'Certainly not!' she snapped, and dropped her pose. 'Surely you don't consider wearing long underwear to be a provocative gesture. I always wear it camping. It's warm and practical.'

Brad walked closer to her and grasped her shoulders with his hands. 'On you, Sara, it's also very sexy.'

She grabbed his arms to push him away, but could only hang on as she felt her legs tremble and weaken. A tiny flame in his eyes flared as he leaned closer, his eyes on her lips. She knew she should say something funny, and slip out of his arms, but she stood hypnotised, and

then it was too late as his lips lightly touched hers, and
her body drew closer to his, and she leaned against him
to draw upon his strength as his mouth drained her very
being. She felt a fire begin to burn in her stomach and
spread throughout her body until she feared it would
consume her. But it was a fire that demanded more and
more, and when Brad's mouth deserted hers, she
moaned and wildly turned her mouth begging his to
return, but he only chuckled softly, and she felt his lips
nibbling her earlobe and then travel around her cheek
and to the base of her neck. She half turned in his arms
and arched her back, silently inviting him to take more
and more of her. Hungrily his lips returned to hers, and
this time it was she who plumbed the depths of his
mouth, seeking and searching. She felt one of his hands
descend to her hips, cradling her close to the hardness
of his thighs. His other hand tried to capture the wildly
beating pulse at the base of her throat and then slowly
his spread fingers caressed her breast. She thought she
flinched away then, only to realise seconds later that she
had urged herself closer to his hand. Momentarily his
hand stilled and then moved upward. Her breast felt
cold and abandoned, and she heard herself give a moan
of disappointment. But now Brad's hand was at her
buttons, and she wiggled closer to him in relief. His
hand left her buttons and gathered in her hair and
pulled her face back so he could look at her. The
flickering light of the lantern threw shadows across his
face, and she could see the reflections of the flame in his
eyes. He looked closely at her face, and she knew the
passion she felt must be reflected in her eyes, but she
was beyond caring. Her mouth was dry, and
unconsciously she licked her lips, her tongue darting
out nervously.

Quickly Brad leaned down and captured her tongue
gently in his teeth, and a sigh shook her body. He
resumed his toying with the buttons, and then cold air
swirled about her as he pushed aside the shoulders of
her long underwear to expose her breasts to his hands

and eyes. She felt her breasts tingle and become warm and heavy while his fingers teased the nipples into hard little nubs. He looked down, and the pink buttons drew his mouth, and ecstasy shattered her as his tongue took over from his fingers. Her hands pressed his head to her breast, and she pushed even closer to him, her fingers raking through his hair. Suddenly he picked her up and carrying her to her sleeping bag, placed her down upon it. He leaned back on his heels, his face taut with need as he looked at her. She was bare to the waist, but she didn't care. Smiling up at him, delighted with her power over him, she slowly stretched, her arms above her head.

'Tell me again you're not being provocative,' Brad said in a thickened voice.

'I can't.' Sara reached up and pulled his mouth down to meet hers.

'Sara!' he groaned, and flung his body down the length of hers.

The wool fabric of his shirt assaulted her tender nipples, but it was only one of the many sensations bombarding her body. She loosed her hands from behind his neck and gently pushed him away. He looked at her questioningly, but she shyly ducked her head and concentrated on the buttons of his shirt, then spread the shirt wide and pulled him back close so that his skin was cool and dry against hers. The shaky beat of his heart sounded a counterpoint to the uneven thud of hers, and she knew he was as lost to passion as she was. She felt his hand slip into her long underwear and caress her thighs. Suddenly cold realisation struck her, and she began to struggle wildly, feeling not the heat of passion, but the heat of shame. 'No!' she cried out in panic.

Brad's hands and mouth abruptly stilled. He raised his head, and his eyes, darkened by passion, searched her face.

Sara frantically tried to roll from beneath Brad's long hard body, but he captured both her hands in one large hand and held them above her head while his other hand stroked her trembling body. 'It's okay, Sara, it's okay. I want you, and you want me—it's as simple as that.'

'No,' she denied.

He raised one eyebrow and deliberately looked the length of her half nude body. With his free hand he touched her lips lightly and then trailed his fingers down her throat and ran them teasingly across her breast.

Sara didn't have to look down to know her body responded to his gentle attack. 'Lust is not enough,' she insisted.

'Is that why you're still a virgin?'

She stiffened. 'What makes you think I am? I suppose my inexperience puts you off,' she challenged.

'Sara, Sara!' Brad shook his head. 'First you say you want to stop, and then you accuse me of not wanting to continue. Make up your mind. Which is it?' His lips drew closer to her. She felt hers part, and a light gleamed in his eyes.

'Stop!' she cried. 'I want to stop!' She let out a shuddering breath, that was half a sob.

Immediately Brad sat up and let go of her arms. He pulled her up into a sitting position and yanking up her long underwear, thrust first one of her arms and then the other into the sleeves, ignoring her futile efforts to fend him off and dress herself. When he had buttoned the last button, he stood up and moved over to the lantern. 'Do you need this any longer?' he asked without turning.

'No.'

Brad picked up the lantern and walked out of the tent.

Shakily Sara climbed into her sleeping bag. Exhausted and drained, she wondered how she would ever make it through this camping trip. Maybe now she wouldn't have to. Probably Brad would want to leave in the morning. She was aware that this thought should cheer her up, but the idea of leaving was somehow depressing. What would her father say? What would everyone think? Just when she and Brad seemed to be getting on so well. She couldn't deny that she'd brought it on herself. Brad had seen her actions as an obvious invitation, and accepted. He was probably used to women making overtures. At thirty-three years of age, it was unlikely he had lived a celibate life. He admitted that he wanted her body. The episode would have meant nothing more to him than the satisfying of his desires.

She lay awake for what seemed hours, but Brad didn't come in. Eventually exhaustion won out, and she fell into a light sleep, troubled by dreams of the war and Brad and Peter and her ideas of the prison camp. Once she cried out, and immediately a voice across the tent said 'It's okay, Sara,' and only then did she fall into a deep sleep.

She awoke to the smell of frying bacon and the shadows of a blowing tree limb flitting across the tent. So much for sunrise pictures, she thought wryly. Something struck the side of the tent, and she jumped before she realised that it was Brad banging the tent wall.

'C'mon, sleepyhead, rise and shine! Breakfast is ready.'

'I may rise, but don't expect me to shine,' Sara grumbled loudly. She wondered how she dared face him this morning.

Brad laughed. 'You'll shine after this breakfast of mine,' he boasted. 'Hurry up, or I'll come in and get you,' he threatened.

Sara hurried. In a few minutes she was seated in her chair looking with awe at the plate that Brad handed her. A small trout wrapped in bacon nestled beside an egg fried to perfection and a mound of crisp brown-fried potatoes. Orange juice and coffee awaited her on the table. 'I can't eat all this,' she protested. 'I just drink coffee for breakfast.'

'Are you trying to hurt the cook's feelings? You eat it, or I'll feed you myself,' Brad warned her.

In spite of the laugh in his voice, Sara could tell by the look in his eyes that he meant every word. Hesitantly she picked at the trout and selected a small morsel. 'Brad, this is delicious!' she said in a surprised voice.

'I'll bet you thought we'd starve on my days to cook,' Brad jeered.

Since that was exactly what Sara had thought, she said nothing. Presently she leaned back in her chair and sipped her coffee contentedly. 'Breakfast was delicious, Brad. I'll even volunteer to do the dishes!'

'There was never any doubt about that,' he replied loftily.

Sara threw her wadded-up napkin at him.

Laughing, he dodged and grabbed her hand. His laughter died out, and he looked seriously at Sara. 'We have to talk.'

'No.' She looked away and tried to retrieve her hand. She didn't want to talk about her humiliation last night, about how she had almost told Brad she loved him. Neither did she want him to suggest they leave.

He firmly grabbed her chin and forced her to face him. 'Sara, about last night. I want to apologise. It was my fault, but I promise you, it won't happen again. Last night things just got out of hand. This is a very romantic setting, with just the two of us thrown together. You're a very desirable woman, Sara, and for a moment I forgot you were Peter's sister.'

'Of course, Peter's sister,' Sara said bleakly. 'And what did I forget?'

Brad looked away. 'The emotion of the place, the time was too much for you, Sara, and you mistook that for something else. Perhaps your father expected too much of you this summer. Bringing you to this valley that holds so many memories of Peter, putting up the pictures, having me here to remind you further, and then your dad coercing you up here.' He laughed dryly at her quick start. 'You think I don't realise that the last place you wanted to come was up here where your memories of Peter are the most intense? And then to have me remind you that it should be Peter up here with you instead of me. That's what really hurts, isn't it? Peter died, and I came home.'

Horrified, Sara tried to shut him up, to deaden the pain she saw in his eyes. 'No, no, Brad, that's not true! I never wished you were dead instead of Peter. Never!'

'I do understand, Sara,' Brad said as he gently smiled at her, as one smiles to reassure a child.

'Listen to me, Brad. I didn't—I don't. Never! You must believe that!' In her anxiety, Sara clutched at his shoulders, squeezing his arms.

He reached over and patted her hand. 'If it's that important to you, then of course I believe you, Sara.' He stood up. 'Since you're doing the dishes, I think I'll try my luck at fishing again. I noticed a promising looking pool in the stream farther down the hill. Okay?'

Sara knew Brad was asking her about more than his going fishing. 'Okay, Brad,' she answered coolly.

Her thoughts were in a turmoil as her hands splashed idly in the quickly cooling dishwater. Brad's words had given birth to a totally new idea for her, and she needed time to think it through. There was a certain amount of truth in his statement that she was hurt because Peter had died and Brad hadn't. But it wasn't the truth as Brad saw it. Suddenly she saw how different things would have been if Peter had returned. She had felt guilty over neglecting Peter for Brad, but was that really why she felt guilty? Wasn't the truth of the matter that she was angry at Peter? Angry at him starting the affair between her and Brad, the long-distance affair that had hurt her so deeply. Then, when she was suffering and needed Peter the most, he had let her down. Instead of coming to her aid, he had died, had, in effect, abandoned her. Sara slowly sat down, pondering this revolutionary idea. Subconsciously she must have realised her anger against Peter and felt guilty. If she acknowledged why she felt guilty, then she acknowledged anger at Peter. Her barely adult mind had not accepted that traitorous idea, and instead she had channelled her guilt into a more acceptable channel. She had blamed herself for forsaking Peter for Brad who was not as worthy as Peter. With painful sharpness she saw how she had fed her guilt through the years.

Coming back to the valley had forced this honesty upon her. Peter was her brother, not a god. In the ordinary scheme of things, she would have met a man and married, and loving Peter would never have been a handicap. A woman needed to love different men in different ways—as a father, a brother, a lover. The telescoping of so many tragic events into such a short period of her life when she had barely outgrown adolescence had twisted her reasoning. Loving Brad as she had not been disloyal to Peter. If Brad had come to her, he would have helped her overcome her grief for Peter. There would have been no feelings of anger, no guilt. If Peter had lived, he would have been there to comfort her when Brad had hurt her, Losing them both had distorted her thinking. It was all so clear now to Sara that she was amazed at how long she had struggled with her guilt. She should have come to the valley before. The valley forced one to confront the truth. Sara had confronted her particular truth, and now a peaceful calm invaded her limbs.

She lay back in the chaise and thought of Brad. He hadn't believed her when she had said she hadn't wanted him dead instead of Peter. How could she convince him without confessing that she loved him? It was one thing to be honest with herself. Exposing her innermost thoughts to Brad was something else again.

Brad had apologised this morning, but behind that apology was a warning. Being Peter's sister had saved her last night, and it would prevent Brad from approaching her, but if she offered again, he was accepting. That was the implication behind his words. Not because he loved her, but because she had been blessed with an attractive body. She loved him. Wouldn't it be better to grab of life what she could? She wanted to touch him, to have him hold her and to touch her. Sara sighed. Was she a fool to have rejected Brad last night? Now he would be kind and gentle and friendly, even like a brother, and she didn't know if she could stand that. How could she make it through a whole week living so intimately with him and yet not intimate at all?

The days passed easier than Sara had anticipated. Brad was a comfortable companion, and she found herself laughing naturally with him. She shared thoughts and ideas as she had not done with anyone since Peter's departure. Some days they stayed together, Brad fishing while Sara read or just watched him and chatted. Other days each went his own way. Brad would want to try the river downstream or up, while Sara's destination would be a particular landscape or field of flowers in the opposite direction. Evenings they met at the campfire where they quietly discussed their days. At night, Sara was careful to keep to her side of the tent and out of Brad's way. For his part, Brad usually waited until she was soundly sleeping until he came into the tent. The second night she had been reluctant to seek her bed, but he had guessed at her hesitation and quickly admonished her not to worry, and the awkward moment had passed.

The emotional events of the first night had not been repeated, and Sara couldn't decide if this omission pleased her or disappointed her. She felt occasional flashes of resentment that Brad could so easily keep their relationship on a strictly friendly basis, while at the same time she was grateful that the lack of opportunity prevented her from betraying her love to him. The wall of friendship between them must be maintained. Lowering of the barriers could only mean Sara would be exposing herself to rejection and humiliation as she had done ten years before.

CHAPTER SIX

SARA lay on her back idly watching the wispy white clouds meander across the blue sky. Gradually the floating clouds lulled her, and she felt her eyes closing. A sudden sharp pain in her stomach aroused her, and she quickly opened her eyes to see a pebble resting on her shirt.

'Hey, lazybones!' Brad's voice hailed her.

She raised herself on one elbow. 'Did you just throw a rock at me?' she asked suspiciously.

He looked at her in wide-eyed innocence. 'Must have been dropped by a passing bird.'

'Sure,' Sara scoffed.

'Listen, as long as you're up, you can do me a favour,' Brad wheedled.

'What?'

'Bait me another hook, will you? I'm not having any luck with these salmon eggs, so I think I'll try worms. Use that other rod.'

Sara grimaced at him, but hauled herself up to do his bidding. The rod was where he had indicated, and she deftly tied a hook on it. Carefully searching in his tackle box, she located a white cardboard container that looked like a cottage cheese box with holes in the lid. She gingerly pried the lid off, using one of Brad's large metal lures. Her nose curled as she surveyed the ugly wiggly brown mass of very large earthworms. She looked around her for a twig or stick, but in vain, as they were above the timberline, and even the few plants were close to the ground with no appreciable amount of stem. She bit her lower lip in frustration. She could not admit her pedicament to Brad. For no amount of money in the world would she tell him that she couldn't bear to touch worms. Slowly her eyes scanned the area

116

about her again, and this time she spied a large flat stone. Using the metal lure to poke and pry into the squirming brown pile, she managed to separate one large worm from the others, and prod him out of the carton on to the rock. She firmly replaced the lid on the container and placed it back in the tackle box. Taking the lure in one hand, she attempted to hold the worm still while she poked the hook into his body, but the worm refused to co-operate and wiggled and flipped about until he had her muttering under her breath.

Brad's amused voice spoke behind her. 'What in the world are you doing?'

Chagrined, Sara eyed him. 'I'm baiting your hook.'

He roared with laughter. 'Do you always bait your hook like that?'

'No,' she said defiantly. 'I usually wear gloves.'

'Gloves!' Brad choked on the words. 'You've got to be kidding.'

Sara's eyes narrowed. 'Peter laughed at me.' She added in an ominously casual voice, 'Only once.'

'I wouldn't be surprised if he laughed more than once,' said Brad, attempting to suppress his laughter.

Sara smiled sweetly. 'Enjoy your mirth.' She stood up and carefully brushed off the seat of her jeans. 'I don't get mad. I just get even,' she promised as she moved off.

Brad was not properly intimidated, she decided, as she heard him giving in to his laughter behind her. Pretending unconcern, she sat down by her pack and picked up her paperback mystery. She feigned interest in it while her mind frantically raced to produce ideas for revenge against Brad for laughing at her.

Brad walked over to her and dropped to his knees. 'If I apologise on bended knee, am I forgiven?'

Sara disdained to answer.

Softly he spoke again. 'Sara, I'm sorry I laughed at you. Please forgive me.'

She sniffed. 'I'll consider it.'

'I guess we all have hang-ups,' he offered in a conciliatory tone.

'Worried about revenge?' Sara taunted.

'No. I just want to make sure we're still friends.'

'Certainly,' she agreed stiffly.

'Sara,' Brad cajoled, 'I'm sorry I laughed, but even you must admit it's an unusual way to bait a hook. You've already admitted it's not even your usual method.' His mouth quivered.

'Brad, if you laugh at me again, I'll ... I'll ... I'll hit you!' Sara threatened.

He drew back in pretended terror. 'Maybe I'd better go back to my fishing and leave you to your book.'

'Yes, I think you'd better.'

Halfway back to the lake, Brad turned around. 'It's easier to read if the book is right side up,' he called.

'Oh, you!' Sara found a clump of grass and threw it in his general direction.

He waved merrily and continued on down to the lake's shore. Sara could see his shoulders shaking and knew he was still laughing at her. She didn't really mind. Brad was such good fun. The book forgotten, she lay down again.

Even in the middle of the summer, snow capped the peaks which surrounded the still waters of the lake. The only movement about her was Brad casting his bait into the water, causing ripples to distort the mirrored images of the mountains. They had climbed together this morning to this high isolated glacier lake. While Brad had fished, Sara had done some hiking and admired and photographed the extensive wildflowers. After a successful morning and a satisfying lunch, she had been catnapping when Brad's pebble had aroused her. The day had been a lazy contented one, and she wished her future promised more days like this with him.

The next morning Brad decided to use his fly rod and work his way downstream from the lake casting into any likely looking pools. Remembering the pleasant time they'd enjoyed the previous day, Sara was tempted to join him, but instead decided to return to a patch of flowers that she had photographed earlier in the week.

The light had been tricky before, and she wasn't sure she'd got the desired results. She decided she had better go back and take some more pictures just to be on the safe side.

Several hours later she stood up and stretched, satisfied with her morning's labours. Walking back to her pack, she pulled out a sandwich and sat contentedly munching it. A shadow fell over her shoulder, and she shivered in the sudden chill. Rain clouds building up along the mountains convinced her that she'd better get back to camp before a summer squall struck.

With one eye on the ominous clouds scudding overhead and one eye on the treacherous rocky hillside, she hurried down towards the camp. At the bottom of the slope, she found she was downstream of the lake and camp, and she decided to follow the stream rather than the trail. Then, if she found Brad, she could walk back to camp with him. A slight movement caught her eye, and she watched with delight as a dipper hopped along the bottom of the river searching for his dinner, while the water rushed over his head. Knowing the little grey bird was perfectly suited to his peculiar food gathering methods, Sara watched in amusement as he caught a small fish and flipped it up on a large rock. The small bird hopped up beside the flopping minnow for several minutes before he succeeded in capturing his prize once again and swallowing it in one gulp. Intent on his dinner, the dipper ignored her passing.

Still smiling as she rounded a bend in the stream, she saw the scene before her unfold in stark contrast. At this point the stream widened, and the trees along the banks pointed up to a wide expanse of sky. The sky was leaden and grey here, not threatening as over the mountains, but bleak and dreary-looking, with that peculiar yellow light that often foretold a storm. At the edge of the stream sat Brad, a cold desolate expression on his face. Whatever his thoughts were, they could not be pleasant ones. Sara hesitated, unsure whether to ignore the droop of his face and shoulders and go up to him with a cheerful quip, or to withdraw silently before he sensed her presence. As she stood, indecisive, she noticed how Brad's posture and expression matched the brooding sky. An idea came to her, and ignoring the ethics of her actions, she snatched up her camera, and fitting on a long-distance lens, proceeded to snap Brad against the stormy background. But the lens was not giving her the nuance of the scene that she sought. Frustrated, Sara knew she would have to change lenses and quietly move closer to Brad. If he saw her, she knew the mood of the scene would be lost. Cautiously, with the new lens in place, she crept up closer to him. She adjusted the camera setting and looked at the suddenly clear image of Brad that came into focus—and almost gasped out loud at the raw suffering visible on his face. The eerie cloud-scudded sky provided the perfect backdrop for features etched with lines of pain and despair. Brad's eyes gazed at nothing, and Sara's heart ached at the distressing scene before her. She bit her upper lip and slowly depressed the shutter. The click sounded like a bomb in the quiet sullen air. Even as she heard it, she knew Brad also did. Startled, he turned and glared at her, and she gulped. Brad was furious, and rightly so. She had no business infringing on his privacy in such a manner. She opened her mouth to apologise.

'Enjoying yourself?' Brad's contemptuous words lashed out at her.

Sara's words turned to ashes in her mouth. Even from this distance she could see the rage in his eyes. 'I . . . I was . . . was just taking . . . taking your picture . . .' she attempted.

'Funny, but I don't remember you asking my permission,' he sneered.

She hesitated. 'I . . . I wouldn't have done anything with it without your permission.'

'Done anything?'

Brad's frigid tones warned her that she was on treacherous ground, but she plunged guiltily ahead. 'I wouldn't have sold it without your permission.'

Brad's face was flinty. 'Do you have the nerve to tell me that you sneaked up on me and took my picture and now you want to sell it?'

'No, no!' Sara cried out in horror. 'You misunderstand.' She was angry at herself. Knowing full well she had been in the wrong, her guilty attempts to appease Brad had given him an entirely erroneous impression.

'Oh, I understand all right. It'll look great in your portfolio. What did you intend to title it? Memories?' he asked furiously.

So he knew how he'd looked. His thoughts had been naked for the world to see, and she had rudely trampled them. What kind of person was she, to be more concerned with a photograph than the man? Why hadn't she resisted the compulsion to take Brad's picture? The way he looked would be for ever imprinted on her mind anyway. She tried again to apologise. 'Brad, I'm sorry. I was way out of line, there's no excuse for what I did. I truly am sorry.' Her voice faltered under his white-hot anger. 'I . . . I won't . . . I won't do anything with the photograph.'

'You certainly won't!' He strode over to her, anger and determination mingling on his face. He reached for her camera.

'Brad, what are you doing?' Sara backed away, her camera held behind her.

'I want that film.'

'No!'

'Yes. Give it to me.'

'Brad, no!' she wailed. 'I spent the whole day up on the mountain taking wildflower photos, and some of them are still in the camera. I promise I'll give you all the prints of you when the film is developed.'

'All? How many did you take, anyway? You little snoop!' He reached for the camera again.

'Brad, please,' Sara pleaded, backing up until a tree behind her forced her to stop. 'I said I'm sorry. I'll give you all the prints. What more do you want?'

'I want that film now,' he muttered between clenched teeth.

Sara cowered. The tree behind her prevented her from backing up any further, and she couldn't slip around it and escape from Brad. He caught up with her and realised her predicament. An arm on either side of her pinned her tight against the tree. She could feel the rough bark of the tree dig into her back. One hand brushed against some sticky sap, but she was only aware of Brad towering menacingly over her.

'Brad, please!' Nervously Sara licked her lips. Before she grasped his intentions, he swiftly bent his head and brutally kissed her. Her head banged back against the tree. She pressed her lips tighter together, but Brad ground his mouth harder on hers, and she tasted a slight tinge of blood. His hips thrust her back hard against the trunk, and she felt her breasts constrained against his hard chest. The entire length of his firm tough body pressed her hard into the rough bark, but she was barely aware of any discomfort as hotter, more disturbing sensations raced through her blood. Her head pounded, her lips throbbed, her heart beat thunderously, and still Brad continued his chastising kiss. Sara felt a small prick in her right breast, and then as Brad stepped back from her, a searing pain tore at her breast, and she almost fainted from the shock of it. She must have staggered, because his muscular arms caught at her and held her upright.

'If you want to dance, you have to pay the piper,' he muttered.

Waves of pain danced before Sara's eyes. 'Here.' Blindly she thrust the camera at Brad and turned in the direction of camp.

'Giving up so easy?' Brad's jeering voice barely penetrated Sara's haze. He grabbed her shoulder.

'Leave me alone,' she mumbled, and she started off in a staggering run towards camp.

Brad let her go, and turned back the other way to where his fishing gear was strewn about.

Around the corner and out of Brad's sight, she stopped and looked down at her breast. Aghast, she discovered the source of the pain. A fish-hook had penetrated her shirt and was now firmly embedded in her breast just inches above the nipple. Hesitantly Sara took hold of the feathered end. Even the slightest touch caused shimmering waves of pain and nausea. She took several deep breaths to clear her head. She knew she had to get back to camp and find the tweezers and first aid kit. She could hear Brad crashing along the trail behind her. Not wanting him to see her, she began to run for camp. Tears of pain blinded her, and she didn't notice the large exposed tree root in front of her. The toe of her boot caught and sent her crashing face down in the middle of the trail. Her arms instinctively shot out to break her fall, and she took the brunt of it on her hands and knees. Shaken, she lay still a minute.

'Sara, are you okay?' Concern for her sharpened Brad's voice as he helped her up. 'I think you just scraped up your palms a little. Your jeans protected your knees. Come on, I'll help you back to camp and wash up your wounds.'

By now her breast was shrieking with pain, and she was near to swooning. Hot tears cascaded down her face.

'Please don't cry, Sara. I'm sorry I was such a brute back there. Please stop crying.'

But Sara was incapable of stopping.

Brad looked at her closely. 'Do you think you broke something, Sara? Is your ankle giving you pain? For heaven's sake, Sara, where does it hurt?' Anxiety lent an impatient edge to his voice.

She could only shake her head as the waves of pain grew more and more intense each passing moment. Brad put his arm around her shoulders to guide her back to camp. The pressure of his arm pulled on her shirt, and she screamed involuntarily at the tearing pain.

'What's wrong, Sara?' Brad cried out.

She felt herself scooped up into his arms, and even

with the pain, she felt a small measure of comfort before all went black around her.

Something warm and moist touched her face. Reluctantly she opened her eyes to see Brad's face close to hers, his eyes dark with concern.

'Sara, I'm so sorry,' he said in a husky voice. 'I'd never hurt you like this on purpose.'

She smiled wanly, still weak from the pain of her throbbing breast. Forcing herself to look down, she saw her blouse was unbuttoned and pulled down over one shoulder. A large white gauze bandage swathed almost the entire breast. She was lying on the chaise-longue with Brad sitting beside her. Even in her pain she was very conscious of the warmth emanating from his hard thighs. He was holding a wet cloth and had evidently been bathing her face. Now he reached for her hands and gently began washing the dirt and grime from them.

'Did I faint?' she asked at last. Anything to break the silence.

'Yes, and it was just as well. Removing a fish-hook is never fun, and in a tender place . . .' The sentence trailed off as Brad renewed his ministrations on her palms.

'Did you have to pull it through and cut it?' she asked in a trembling voice.

'No,' he answered. 'There's a new method where you press on the hook and can pull it out where it went in. It doesn't tear up the skin so much, but it still hurts like the holy dickens.'

Sara lightly touched her wound. 'You're telling me,' she said wryly.

Brad busied himself with smoothing a salve on her hands. 'I suppose this means I'm chief cook and bottlewasher now.'

Sara tried to grin. 'Every cloud has a silver lining.' She shifted in her chair and grimaced as a pain shot through her chest.

'Bad?' Brad asked sympathetically.

She nodded. 'Bad enough.' She bit her lip at the pain.

'At least I had a tetanus shot before I came to Colorado. Old habits die hard.'

'Old habits?'

'Yes. Dad always insisted we kids get tetanus boosters regularly because we spent so much time running around the woods and mountains. This is the first time I've ever needed one.'

'Actually,' said Brad, 'you probably don't need one now. I'd never used that hook.'

'I don't understand where it came from,' Sara said.

'My fishing vest,' he answered. 'There's a furry strip across the front for extra hooks, and I had several stuck in there. Not stuck firmly enough, I'm afraid.' He looked directly into her face. 'Sara, I want to apologise.'

She quickly pressed her fingers on his lips. 'No, Brad. I was trespassing, and you were justifiably angry.'

'I had no right to lose my temper and maul you like that, no matter what I thought you'd done. This is all my fault,' he said as he indicated her wound.

'It wasn't. Let's just forget it, okay?' she murmured. She didn't feel like any discussions right at the moment.

'Poor Sara! You don't feel so chipper, do you?'

Sara wished Brad would go away and leave her alone. Her hands burned, her knees throbbed, and most of all, her breast flamed with pain. It strained her control to keep from bursting into tears again.

The anticipated storm had not materialised, but the evening chill was setting in, and she shivered. Immediately Brad stood up and left. Perversely, now that he had done as she'd wished, Sara wanted him back, and she felt miserable. Tears were welling up, and she closed her eyes in a fruitless effort to hold them in.

'Poor Sara,' Brad's voice said soothingly from near by. 'It's the pain and the shock. I washed the wound well, and put on a disinfectant, but I'm afraid all the pain pills we have are aspirin. Here, stand up, and I'll tuck you in this for warmth.'

Sara looked up to see him standing by her chair with

her sleeping bag. He helped her up, and with one hand
holding her securely to his side, with the other he flung
her sleeping bag out on the chaise-longue. He helped
her settle in it and then tucked it around her legs and
zipped it halfway up. Then he disappeared into the tent
and came out carrying her chamois shirt. Sitting beside
her, he gently helped her remove her torn and bloody
shirt and helped her on with the chamois one. Carefully
he put the armholes over her skinned-up hands and
tugged the shirt up over her shoulders. Sara was slightly
embarrassed at not wearing a bra, but only had the
energy to snuggle into the soft warm cosiness of the
shirt as Brad gently brought the front edges together
and buttoned her up. She leaned back against the chair
and weakly smiled her thanks, her eyes closing. She felt
him lean closer, and a soft kiss brushed her cheek. 'Not
a fly?' she asked in a drowsy voice.

Brad chuckled. 'No. You rest while I fix some
dinner.'

She was succumbing to the drowsy waves of pain
when he touched her shoulder. 'Here, take two aspirin
and drink this water.' She swallowed the pills and
sipped at the water. 'Drink it all,' he ordered.

'Tyrant,' she muttered weakly as she obediently
downed the whole glass of water.

Satisfied, Brad took the empty glass away.

The pain was too intense for Sara to fall asleep, but
she lay lethargically on the chaise listening to the
evening noises. A grey jay was squawking overhead to
Brad to toss up some choice titbits, while from a near-by
tree, a chickaree scolded them for being in his territory.
Chipmunks squeaked at each other as they scurried
about collecting their dinner. The sounds of nature
mingled with the sounds of Brad cooking. Cutlery
rattled, dishes clattered, and once she heard the crash of
dropping skillets followed by soft curses from Brad.
Soon the smells of frying steak blended with the odour
of the wood fire. Sara sat quietly beside the fire, half in
and out of a cloudy haze of pain and dizziness.

Brad brought her some dinner and insisted on cutting up her meat and feeding her like a baby. She wasn't hungry, but he patiently offered her all the food on her plate, and to her surprise, she managed to eat every bit.

After dinner she rested while Brad did the dishes, then he pulled up his chair and sat silently beside her. She sensed his frequent glances at her. The pain in her chest had settled into one giant intolerable throb, and she felt she couldn't stand it much longer. The night seemed colder, and in spite of her efforts not to do so, she shivered.

Brad immediately stood up and moved over to her and looked down. 'Bedtime for you, I think.'

'Yes,' she agreed, and began to unzip her bag.

'No need to do that,' he said, and leaning down, he picked her up, sleeping bag and all, and holding her close to his chest, carried her into the tent and laid her down on her foam camping pad. 'How about two more aspirin?'

Weakly she nodded.

She didn't think she'd be able to sleep, but aided by the aspirin, at last she fell into an uneasy slumber. Whimpering sounds awakened her. She lay shivering in her sleeping bag wondering what animal was in pain. Her whole chest throbbed in agony, her teeth were chattering, and she was shaking from the pain and cold. If only the whimpering would stop! It made her feel worse.

A rustling from the other side of the tent told her that Brad was also awake. A dark shadow detached itself from the tent wall and came towards her. 'Sara, is it pretty bad?' he asked in a commiserating tone.

Suddenly Sara realised the whimpering came from her. She blurted out, 'It hurts,' and was immediately ashamed to be so childish.

Brad leaned down and lightly pressed his palm on her forehead. 'I think you have a little chill. Reaction mingled with the pain, I'd guess.' He turned away, and she felt more miserable than ever. Then he was back, dragging his sleeping bag. He unzipped her bag and laid it flat. Placing his bag over hers, he zipped up one side and the bottom, making one large double bag. He crawled in beside her and zipped up the other side.

Sara felt too wretched to even ask his intentions.

He rolled over close to her and pulled her body to lie the length of his. His arm around her waist pulled her back in tight to his chest. 'Do you feel warmer now, Sara?' he breathed in her ear.

Sara nodded weakly. While still in great pain, she could feel the heat of Brad's body seeping into hers, and at last drowsiness and warmth won out over pain, and she slept.

Once, during the night, she partially awakened and stirred, but Brad's voice soothingly told her to go back to sleep, and to her surprise, she did.

When she woke, the sun was shining and tree shadows danced across the top of the tent. Smells of frying bacon tantalised her nose, and she sharply regretted that this was their last morning in camp. Gingerly she moved. Her breast still ached, but it had settled to a manageable throb. Her hands were stiff and awkward, but by moving carefully she was able to change into clean clothing.

'Everything okay in there?' Brad had evidently heard her stirring.

'I don't feel like jogging, but I'll live.'

He chuckled. 'Well, hurry up, Breakfast is ready.' He eyed her critically as she emerged from the tent. 'You look better. Let me see your hands.'

Obediently Sara extended them, palms up.

'They look pretty good. Apparently we got all the dirt and gravel out. Are they very sore? Can you feed yourself this morning?'

'I can manage.'

'Brave Sara,' Brad said lightly, then taking her hands he dropped a light kiss on each of the scratched reddened palms.

Sara snatched her hands back. His kisses had set off fiery little darts up and down her spine. She didn't want him kissing her hands. If she were honest, she'd admit she wanted his kisses in places other than on her hands. Brad was being kind and gentle to her, treating her as he would a small child or a wounded animal. She must remember this and not embarrass them both by responding with love and passion to his kind gestures.

Brad handed her a plate, and shakily she sat down to eat. The food was probably delicious, but tasted like sawdust to her, and she could barely swallow it. Finally she forced herself to ask the question, 'When do you want to break camp and leave?'

Brad tossed her a quick glance. 'I suppose I may as well wash up these dishes and begin packing. up. Did you want to take any more pictures?'

Sara gave a negative shake of her head.

'I think I've fished enough to last me a while.' He looked at her plate. 'Through?' he asked as he reached for it. 'You can sit there and relax. I'll take care of loading up.'

She surveyed her damaged palms ruefully. 'I guess I wouldn't be much help, would I?'

Brad began gathering up the dishes preparatory to washing them. Sara leaned back in her chair and watched him. A wave of longing coursed over her, startling her with its intensity. Brad was so good-looking. His grey hair, scars and lined face accentuated his masculinity. Sara was reminded of the models on the old smoking advertisements. He had about him that same aura of rugged masculinity, rock-hard strength and virility which all added up to great sex appeal. Not only a man that men could like and respect, he was a man that women would long to belong to. Sara caught her breath. Oh, how she longed to be Brad's, to be in his arms and give herself solely and totally to him. Lost in her dreams, at first she didn't see Brad standing in front of her. 'Did you say something to me?'

'Daydreaming?' he smiled, and Sara wondered if he realised about whom she was dreaming.

'No,' she lied. 'Just memorising the fleecy white clouds tumbling through the blue sky, the tall pines, the shimmering lake ...' The words caught in her throat. 'It's so beautiful—I hate to leave.'

'Beautiful,' Brad agreed, his eyes never leaving Sara's face.

Sara blushed. She hated herself for doing it, but could not prevent the warm flush she felt creeping up her neck, even though she knew that he was merely teasing her.

He gave a soft laugh, then sat down on the edge of her chair. 'I need to change your bandage.' He'd been carrying the first aid kit, and now opening it, he handed the small metal case to Sara.

She took it, but with the other hand convulsively clutched the front of her shirt together. 'I can do it!' she squeaked.

Brad brushed aside her hand and unbuttoned her shirt. 'You can barely see it from your angle without a mirror. I'm just going to change the bandage. I'll try not to hurt,' he added in a reassuring voice.

Hurt her! Sara thought hysterically. That had never entered her mind. It was touching her that she didn't think she could stand. She held herself stiffly as Brad exposed the injured breast. He carefully kept the other breast covered. Gently he tugged at the bandage, and Sara winced at the shooting pain.

'I'll be as quick as I can,' he promised.

'I'll be brave, Daddy,' Sara retorted in a mock little girl's voice.

'Looks good.' He sat back and surveyed the wound with satisfaction.

She couldn't bring herself to look. 'Do you think it will scar?'

'It shouldn't. It's only a small puncture wound.'

'Small?' Sara yelped. 'It feels like a crater!'

Brad laughed as he deftly taped on a new dressing. 'I don't think it will upset any of your lovers,' he teased.

'Would it upset you?' Sara asked wistfully.

'Do my scars bother you?' he countered.

'I hate them!' she said fiercely, thinking how sick she felt at the thought of Brad's suffering at the time he had received his scars.

His face closed. In a voice devoid of emotion, he said, 'Then I must make sure you aren't offended by them any more.' He snapped shut the first aid kit, stood up and stiffly walked away. 'You can button up your shirt now.' The cold words came back over his shoulder.

Open-mouthed, Sara stared at his departing back. 'Brad, I'm sorry. I didn't mean . . . that's not . . . you don't understand . . .' Her words floundered in her distress. She stood up and started towards him. 'Brad,' she grabbed at his arm.

He shook her off and then looked over her head. 'Company's coming—button up your shirt. Braless may be sexy, but not with a bandage like that.'

The harsh words were like a slap in the face, and Sara flinched at the contempt in Brad's voice. Angry at the interruption, she buttoned her shirt with clumsy fingers. Once again Brad had misinterpreted her words, but now there wasn't time to explain. Besides, he had disappeared into the tent.

With a shower of pebbles, a dark blue van skidded into camp, raising a cloud of dust. Josh grinned from the driver's seat, while Christy scrambled out of the other front door. And following her out was—no! Sara wiped her eyes in disbelief. Out stepped Ces, immaculate in designer jeans, not a speck of dust on her ruffled cowgirl shirt, and every hair in place. Immediately Sara was aware of her own mussed clothing and hair that had only been washed in the lake. She longed for her tub at home. Idiot, she jeered at herself, who's even noticing how you look? She tried to put pleasure into her voice. 'Well, well, look who's here! Welcome to our humble abode.' She made a low theatrical bow. 'Are you here to fetch us home?'

'What a drive!' Josh shuddered dramatically, ignoring her question.

'What a gorgeous place!' Christy enthused, giving Sara an exuberant bear-hug. 'I'd forgotten how beautiful it is.'

Sara almost fainted from the pain, but managed to paint a smile on her face and not cry out.

Josh looked at her keenly. 'What happened to your hands?' he demanded, and grabbed them and inspected the palms. 'I thought they were all healed after that river episode.'

'Sara!' Christy was horrified at the raw red palms. 'What have you been doing to yourself up here? Don't tell me you went swimming again?' she teased.

'I became very intimate with the local soil,' Sara joked.

Christy glared at Brad. 'I'd think you could take better care of Sara than that.'

'Christy!' Sara was shocked at her sister's attack on Brad. 'It had nothing to do with Brad. I'm a big girl and I can take care of myself,' she added defiantly, avoiding meeting Brad's eyes.

'You're right, Christy,' Brad injected smoothly. 'I didn't keep a close enough eye on Sara. I guess I'm just a lousy babysitter.'

'Why . . . why, you . . .' Sara spluttered indignantly.

At that moment Ces, who had been wandering about the camp, disappeared into the tent. Sara caught her breath in dismay. It was bad enough that they'd been caught sharing the tent, but what would Ces think when she saw the two sleeping bags zipped into one double bed? Sara could only imagine the conclusions that Ces would immediately jump to. Ces emerged from the tent, but Sara could discern no visible signs of emotion on her face.

Perplexed, she turned to see Brad watching her, amusement flitting across his face. Still looking at her, he raised his voice so that Josh over by the van could hear him. 'Since you're here, Josh, maybe you'll help me pack up since Sara can't. The sleeping bags are rolled and ready to load. Mine is out here by the tent.'

Sara was grateful for Brad's quick thinking and even quicker actions. In relief she let out the breath she'd been holding. She turned to Christy again. 'Why are you here?' she asked.

'Josh has the day off and wants to do some back-country fishing. This is on our way, so we stopped to say "howdy". Do you want to go with us? It should be gorgeous up there.'

The thought of bouncing over rough trails with her tender breast made Sara queasy. But before she could decline the invitation, Ces spoke up.

'Yes, Sara, you go with Christy and Josh. I'll help Brad clean up here and keep him company on the trip home. We won't need you.'

Even then Sara would have gone with Brad and Ces if Brad hadn't picked that moment to exert his authority. 'Sara is going home with us, Ces.'

Ces sniffed. 'If you think we need a chaperone . . .'

Sara stiffened indignantly. She could make up her own mind. 'I believe I will go with Josh and Christy. Sounds like fun. Do you have enough lunch for me?' she inquired with spurious interest. 'I'll just toss my camera gear in the back here.'

Brad stalked over to where Sara was loading her things into Josh's van. 'Don't be a little fool, Sara. You know you're in no condition to go ramming about the countryside. Be sensible and come with Ces and me.'

'I wouldn't want to be a chaperone,' Sara said in dulcet tones.

Brad laughed. 'That rankled, did it? Don't be an idiot, and give me your things.' He reached for her camera gear.

'Leave it alone!' Sara hissed. 'I'm fine, and I'm going with Christy and Josh.'

'Sara, you are the most exasperating woman I know!'

Ces came up behind them. 'Darling, let Sara do as she wants. You've been stuck with her all week, and Sara is smart enough to know we want to spend some time alone.'

Brad ignored Ces. 'Sara, you're coming with us.'

'No, darling,' Sara mimicked, 'Sara is smart enough to know you two want to be alone.'

'If I didn't know better, I'd almost think you were jealous,' he drawled softly. In the next second his voice cracked like a whip. 'I'm not asking you, I'm telling you, you're going back with me!'

Before Sara could hotly contest Brad's orders, Ces spoke up. 'Perhaps she doesn't like sharing you with me,' she suggested shrewdly.

Ces's astuteness sent a cold chill down Sara's spine. She couldn't let Brad suspect. 'Darling,' she cooed with false sweetness, 'this way I won't have to look at your scars.'

Without a word, Brad turned and walked away.

Sara was sickened by her own cruelty. She wanted to run to Brad, take his face between her hands and kiss away the pain she had heartlessly inflicted.

But Ces's arm on hers stopped her. 'Do they bother you, too?' Ces asked. 'I didn't think they would, you're usually so tenderhearted. I just close my eyes and try to pretend they don't exist.'

Sara just stared at her cousin. Nausea rose in waves and choked at her throat. Jerking her arm from Ces's grasp, she climbed into Josh's van. 'I'm ready when you are,' she called to Christy and Josh in a strangled voice.

Darkness covered the valley when Josh at last parked his van in front of the veranda. Sara had long since given up trying to converse with Christy and Josh and had surrendered to the pulsating pain in her breast. Wearily she contemplated manoeuvring her stiff body out of the van and up the many steps to the room.

Suddenly the car door jerked open. 'Have a nice day?' Brad spat out the words.

Sara looked at him, but no snappy words came. Instead, to her dismay, tears cascaded down her cheeks.

Brad shook his head. 'Not a nice day,' he answered sarcastically, and roughly lifted her out of the car.

His harsh words hammered at her already pain-muddled mind, and she cried harder. Josh and Christy stared at her in astonishment, and weeping uncontrollably, she buried her head in Brad's shirt front.

Cradling her to his chest, Brad carried her up the veranda stairs. He kicked open the door and carried her into the dark entryway.

'What's wrong with Sara?' She heard the concern in her father's voice.

'She's just tired,' Brad answered. 'She shook herself up in a fall yesterday—no, nothing broken, but she had no business going with Josh and Christy today.'

'Brad, what are you doing with Sara?' Sara heard Ces's voice asking shrilly, and then heard her father murmuring as Brad continued on up the stairs. He paused momentarily at Sara's bedroom door, then went inside, pushing the door closed behind him. Still holding her, he went over to the rocking chair and sat down with her held tight in his arms. He had not spoken to her since he had helped her from the van.

Sara knew she should stand up, but she couldn't seem to do anything but cry. She was so weary. Her body ached. She hated herself for making Brad think his scars were disgusting. His dislike for her was clearly demonstrated by the manner in which he had shouted at her when they had driven up. Then why was he sitting here holding her? Didn't he realise how much comfort Sara derived from being in his arms? Was he being kind, or was he only trying to spare her father the sight of a distraught daughter? If she were Ces, he would be murmuring consoling words of love to her now, Sara thought bitterly, not sitting as if carved from stone. She cried harder.

At last her sobs died away, and she sat weakly hiccuping. 'I never cry, but that seems to be all I've done this summer.' A large white handkerchief was poked at her, and she sat up and wiped her eyes and defiantly blew her nose long and loudly. Concentrating on Brad's top shirt button, she said, 'I suppose you're waiting to say, "I told you so".'

'Consider it said,' he answered in a clipped voice.

'Brad, about your scars——' Sara spoke tentatively.

Brad stiffened.

Just then a sharp rap on the door preceded Ces's entrance into the room. 'What are you two doing cuddling here in the dark?' she asked as she snapped on the lights.

Instinctively Sara hid her tear-stained face in Brad's shirt.

'Turn out the lights,' he ordered curtly.

'Pardon me,' Ces snapped in an offended voice as she flipped the light switch.

Sara sighed with relief, having regained the sanctuary of the darkness.

'I just came to give Sara her messages,' Ces said.

'Messages?' Sara asked.

'Your boy-friend called several times.'

'What boy-friend?' Sara asked, her mind still fogged by her crying jag.

'You don't have that many that you should forget him,' Ces said cruelly. 'Roger.'

'Roger? What did he want?'

'You mean there really is a Roger?' asked Brad.

Sara felt his arms drop away, and she willed herself to stand up. 'Yes, of course there is.'

'Do you know this Roger character?' Brad turned to Ces.

'How could I not? He's always hanging around our apartment. I've advised Sara to hold out for marriage. Roger is an extremely wealthy catch,' Ces added in a cloying voice.

'I'm tired. I'd like to go to bed.' Sara abruptly changed the subject.

'Come on, Brad,' Ces gave a high tinkly laugh, 'let's leave Sara to her sweet dreams of young love.'

Brad unfolded his tall body from the chair. 'Are you okay now, Sara?' he asked gravely.

'Fine,' she answered in a falsely cheerful voice.

He stopped in the doorway and was silhouetted

against the hall light. 'Want Christy to come up and help you get into bed?'

'No, thank you.' Sara just wanted to be alone.

'Come on, darling, leave the child to get some sleep,' Ces insisted. She tucked her arm in Brad's and tugged him down the hall, the door swinging shut behind them.

Sara stuck her tongue out at the closing door. Some day she was going to speak up and put Ces in her place! That Ces's place appeared more and more likely to be Brad's arms, she refused to acknowledge.

Slowly she undressed for bed and lowered her aching body on to the cool clean sheets. How heavenly it felt to be in a real bed again! Guiltily she recalled her earlier intention to invite Roger to come out to the valley. She wondered what he wanted, but her eyelids refused to stay open long enough for her to consider the question.

The next morning Sara felt a little stiff, but better equipped to face the world. In the tub the clean warm water sluiced over her body washing away the dirt and easing the aching of her muscles. Stepping out, she towelled herself briskly and then catalogued her injuries. Her hands had lost most of their stiffness and didn't appear nearly as scratched. She removed the wet bandage and was relieved to see the puncture wound was small and healing nicely. A small bandage stuck on it and a bra should keep it clean.

Later, fully dressed, she descended the stairs for breakfast. It was wonderful what a good night's sleep and a hot bath could do for one's morale she thought. The phone rang as she reached the hall, and she picked up the receiver. 'Hello?'

'Sara?' Roger's familiar baritone boomed from the phone.

'Roger—hello,' she answered.

'Miss me?' he teased.

'Sure,' she prevaricated. 'I was just thinking about you.' Her conscience twinged at the small lie. 'I ... I was hoping you could come out for a few days.'

'Sara, I wish I could.' His voice echoed regretfully

over the wires. 'But a special job has come up, and things are really in a turmoil here rushing to meet the deadline. There's no way I can get away now.'

'Oh,' Sara replied in a little voice.

'If I'd have known, but you were so adamant that you didn't want me out there . . .' he chided.

'I know. I'm sorry I was so ugly before I left.'

'Don't worry about it,' came back Roger's comforting words. 'I know how you dreaded the trip. 'How's the vacation coming? Having a good time?'

The trials and tribulations of the past two weeks flashed through Sara's mind, but she knew she couldn't tell him about them. 'Having a lovely time, thank you.'

'Good, good. I hesitated to call, but an assignment came up that I thought you'd like to have a chance at. We need some chipmunk pictures for a layout, and I immediately thought of you out there in the wilderness. There are chipmunks out there, I assume?'

Sara laughed, knowing how Roger was a total city person. 'Yes, Roger, there are.'

'Wonderful! I knew you'd have your camera along. We don't need the photos until next month, but I thought you could be looking for good situations, and when you get back we'll see if you have anything that we can use. Freelance rates, of course, since you're officially on vacation,' he hastened to add.

'Really, Roger? I'd love to, and thanks for calling me about it,' she said eagerly.

'Well, I knew you were getting sick of photographing lemon pies, and I thought this might give you a chance to branch out. Okay?'

'Okay? It's fantastic! How sweet of you to think of me. If you were here, I'd kiss you!'

'That's an invitation almost too good to refuse! I'll take a rain check on it for when you return. What's that?'

Sara could hear Roger talking to someone in the background, then he returned to the phone. 'Listen,

Sara, my secretary just came in. Have to run—some
problem has cropped up.'

'Roger, thanks again. I love you for it.'

'I'd rather you loved me for me,' Roger said wryly as
he rang off.

Sara sighed as she hung up the phone. Knowing her
love for Brad was hopeless, should she settle for
security and companionship with Roger? Was it enough
that Roger loved her? It was like him to sense her
dissatisfaction with her job and help her to make a
change. He was such a good person. She really didn't
deserve his love. Immersed in her thoughts, she didn't
hear Brad's approach.

'A call from the wealthy boy-friend?' His voice
nastily underlined 'wealthy'.

'Yes, that was Roger.'

'His first call in two weeks. He must miss you
terribly,' Brad commented.

Sara ignored the sarcasm. 'Yes, he does,' she replied
coolly. 'He called with a marvellous suggestion about
work. I must go tell Dad about it.' She sped off, barely
noticing Brad staring after her.

CHAPTER SEVEN

SARA didn't see much of Brad for the next couple of days. He was busy pounding his typewriter keys, and although he came to dinner, Sara sensed that his thoughts were back at the cabin with his book. She was relieved to have this respite. She knew now that she loved Brad, but her head swam as she contemplated all the problems. How did Brad feel about Ces? Evidently he enjoyed her company, but on the other hand, Sara didn't think that Brad was missing Ces while they'd been camping. Ces, Sara was certain, might have her eye on Brad, but she didn't love him. And what about Roger?

Much as Sara wanted to forget the past, it existed. Why had Brad never contacted her? Several times he had indicated that he thought Peter's death was a barrier even to friendship between him and Sara. Was it his barrier, or did he think it was hers? Was it impossible for Brad to think of her as a woman instead of just as Peter's kid sister?

Then there were the scars. Sara knew it was her fault that Brad believed that his scars revolted her. She had always been quick to strike out in anger, and as usual, this habit had come back to haunt her. When Brad had hurt her, she had wanted to hurt him back. Ever since the cruel words had left her lips she had regretted them, but the opportunity to take them back had not arisen.

Sara sighed. Even if all the misunderstandings between her and Brad were cleared up, that didn't mean that Brad would love her. What a fool she was to love a man who didn't return her love! She was certainly getting her own back now. In the past, men had loved her, but she had not loved them and had only felt

140

vaguely sorry, but not guilty, because she had never encouraged them. Truth to tell, they had always accused her of being a cold fish. Well, Brad hadn't encouraged her either, and now she was remembering how agonising rejection could be.

Indecision made Sara's head whirl. She couldn't just walk up to Brad and say, 'Listen, I love you. How do you feel about me?' Could she? No, definitely not. For a self-labelled liberated woman, Sara was having a remarkably difficult time managing her love affair. She passed the days in a turmoil of uncertainty and restlessness and was glad to have the chipmunk assignment to occupy her time, if not her mind.

Meanwhile, Ces was working hard at her courtship. The few times that Brad did surface from the cabin, she monopolised his arm and his time, treating him with a patronising yet possessive air that infuriated Sara. She assumed that she herself was successfully hiding her jealous feelings, until one evening Christy had hissed in her ear, 'Either give Ces a run for her money, or get that hangdog expression off your face!' Sara had been too chagrined to even try to deny the implications of Christy's statement, and had ignored her sister's sympathetic yet, 'I told you so', glances.

The following day Sara had looked at her calendar and realised that she had little more than a week of her vacation remaining. She had to do something about Brad, or time would run out on her. She went about the house in a daze, her vacillating thoughts making her head ache. By dinner that evening, she still had no concrete plans, her headache had grown into a dull roaring throb, and she knew she looked terrible as she sat down at the table.

Her father inspected her closely. 'Are you feeling well, Sara? You look pale.'

'I was probably out in the sun too long,' she answered evasively. 'I'll be okay after a good night's sleep.' To change the subject, she turned to Brad. 'How's the book coming?' she asked politely.

'Great. I'm almost done,' he answered. 'In fact, I'm going up to Denver tomorrow to see my publisher. I plan to drive over to Aspen and rent a plane. I'll fly up in the morning, take care of my business and come back that night.'

'I didn't know your publisher was from Denver,' the Judge commented.

'He's not. He's going to be there for some convention, and he wants to discuss a few details with me.'

'I envy you, a day spent in Denver. If only I could go!' Ces hinted broadly.

Brad looked around the table. 'That's a good idea. Let's all go. We can hit the bright lights tomorrow night and fly back on Sunday. How does that sound to you, sir?' he turned courteously to the Judge.

'Twenty years ago I'd have thought it was a wonderful idea. But, at my age, the brights are too bright, I'm afraid. No, you children go, and I'll stay here and enjoy the peace and quiet. The house in Denver is closed up, but you could stay at a hotel.'

'Now, Judge,' Ces drawled, 'I'm sure Sara and Christy won't want you to stay alone. Christy can't leave Josh anyway.'

'I won't,' Christy boldly asserted. 'It's the weekend, so Josh can get away. He can come, too, can't he?' she appealed eagerly to Brad.

'Sure, the more the merrier. Sara's coming, too. She's going to get in a rut if we don't give her a little shove now and again.'

'No, Ces is right. I'll stay and keep Dad company.'

'No, you will not, Sara,' the Judge ordered firmly. 'As accident-prone as you've been all this summer, you go along so Brad can keep an eye on you. Besides, I'd forgotten how noisy you girls are. It will be a good opportunity for me to rest up and prepare to endure the rest of your vacation.'

'Well, I like that!' Sara gasped. 'I didn't realise what a disturbance I've been!'

Her father merely grinned and patted her indignant face. 'Have a good time.'

Sara started to explode, then she noticed the faces around her. Ces was sulky, Christy was watchful, her father was anxious and Brad was expectant. It occurred to Sara that the latter three were waiting for her to make a fuss. Hastily she swallowed her words and smiled sweetly around the table. 'All right, if you're sure you'll be okay here with just Mrs Collins, I'd love to go.' She pressed her napkin over her mouth to keep from laughing at the thunderstruck faces.

In the morning, Sara was torn between happy anticipation of the trip and glum realisation that she'd be a fifth wheel. She sat in the back seat of Josh's van by the window, while Ces sat in the middle between Sara and Brad. Sara couldn't help not notice the way Ces's hand kept straying to Brad's knee. Once Christy turned from the front seat to fling a comment to those at the back, and she gave Sara a disgusted look when she noticed Ces inching closer to Brad. As if I can stop them, Sara thought indignantly. Besides, Brad didn't seem to mind.

She wrenched her thoughts away from the adjoining pair and looked out of the window. They were ascending Independence Pass. A rocky wall rose forbiddingly on her side. The last vestiges of melted snow appeared in crevices, and the thundering waterfalls of early summer had become mere trickles of water. Here and there the blue columbine waved in the breeze. Lavender daisies, yellow sunflowers and coral Indian paintbrush covered the hillsides like dots of children's paints. Josh slowed to manoeuvre around a sharp curve, and Sara smiled to see tourists playfully belting each other with snowballs gathered from a huge dirty patch of snow on the north face. At last they came out of the trees and reached the cold and windswept pass. A small lake, which appeared each summer from the melting snow, shimmered in the pale morning light. Tracks on the hills near the road gave evidence of late spring skiing. Many times in the past Sara had watched foolhardy skiers come tearing down the icy snow to come to grief on a rocky patch or, farther down, to catch a ski on the abundant willow bushes. Today there were only the many tourists taking pictures and gazing at the view, many of them ignoring the signs and walking on the fragile tundra. As they passed the tourist parking area, a new mountain range came into glorious view. The road down was dangerously narrow, and Sara was glad Josh's capable hands were steering them around the steep blind curves. A sharp bark on the left alerted them to the presence of a yellow-bellied marmot. A glimpse was all they had before he dived abruptly over the highway's rim. The ghost town of Independence, formerly a bustling mining community, was quickly passed by, the intriguing old buildings and mine-shafts stark silhouettes against the blue sky. To Sara, so enthralled with the gorgeous scenery along this particular highway, the trip was much too short, and soon they were entering Aspen.

Ordinarily Aspen was very appealing to her, and she loved to browse among the unique and enticing shops. Today, however, the airport was their goal, and they swept through the town barely noticing the Victorian homes or the ski-lift rising up from the town on their left.

At the airport Brad disappeared inside a hanger to discuss final arrangements about the plane he had rented earlier by phone. Josh and Christy meandered about conversing softly and pretending to look over the tethered planes near by.

Restlessly, Sara got out of the van and leaned against the bonnet, gazing up into the surrounding mountains. She was dimly aware of Ces joining her.

'Sara, I want to talk to you.'

Ces's tone of voice rang warning bells in Sara's mind. 'About what?' she asked cautiously.

'Tonight. I don't want you tagging along with Brad and me. You stay with Josh and Christy,' Ces ordered.

Sara looked at Ces in disbelief. 'I thought we were all going out together,' she blurted.

Ces carefully inspected her glossily polished fingernails. 'Brad said his publisher will probably insist on joining us for dinner, and Brad wants me to meet him. I wouldn't want you feeling like an extra body.'

'Which I wouldn't be with Christy and Josh?' Sara asked sarcastically, indicating her sister and Josh, head to head, oblivious of all around them.

'I'm sure the hotel has room service,' Ces said bluntly.

Sara walked away angrily. Why had she let her father talk her into this humiliating situation anyway? Brad and Ces didn't want her, and said so. As for Christy and Josh—well, they wouldn't want her either, but would be too kind to say so. Mentally she ticked off her list of friends in Denver to see whom she could contact. She'd think of someone. If she had to make up an engagement for the evening, she certainly wouldn't shove in where she wasn't wanted.

The plane trip to Denver passed in a haze for Sara. She was vaguely aware of a smooth take-off and a feather-like landing. Engrossed in her thoughts, she paid no attention to the conversation around her.

A rental car awaited them at the Denver terminal, and Brad hustled them all into the vehicle. 'I have hotel reservations downtown at the Brown Palace—hope that's okay. It's centrally located for my business and for your shopping.'

Everyone concurred, and the car bore them down the interstate and then through the busy metropolitan streets to the imposing brown hotel.

'I'll let you all off there and tend to my business. Why don't we plan to meet in the old lobby at seven?' Brad suggested.

Sara remained silent waiting for Ces or Josh to counter the idea, but to her surprise, Josh quickly agreed. 'Seven o'clock sharp, and dressed to kill,' he said.

Sara muttered about other plans, but Christy interrupted.

'Nonsense! It's always been the plan that we do the town together tonight. Don't be a spoilsport, Sara,' Christy ordered.

Sara opened her mouth indignantly to deny that she was a spoilsport when she noticed Brad watching her in the rear view mirror.

Ces sweetly spoke on Sara's behalf. 'Really, Christy, you mustn't interfere with Sara's plans. She has her own life to lead, and you can't tag after her for ever.'

'Well, I like that!' Christy retorted. 'You know darn well that you don't want Sara to go with us because . . .'

'Christy,' Sara hastily interjected, 'I just remembered. I can go with you tonight, after all.' She was sure that Brad was laughing at her.

Brad pulled up in front of the hotel and idled the engine while Josh removed the luggage. As Sara started across the sidewalk towards the massive hotel doors, Brad called her back to the car. Leaning across the front seat, he asked chattily, 'Why does Christy think Ces doesn't want you to come with us?'

Sara blushed in confusion. 'Christy has an active imagination.'

Brad laughed softly. 'I'm looking forward to tonight. Dance with me?'

She looked away, but nodded, then abruptly turned and almost ran into the hotel. Was Brad just flirting, or was it possible that he did care for her at least a little?

As expected, Ces was waiting for her, an angry look on her face. 'I thought I told you to disappear!' she hissed.

'I tried,' Sara insisted.

'Not very hard,' Ces snapped. 'If you think you're going to win Brad away from me like you did Roger, think again! Brad is going places, and he needs a wife who can keep up. He certainly doesn't want some dewy-eyed country girl who looks more at home in hiking boots than evening heels!'

Before Sara could reply, Christy walked up and dangled the room keys. Ces grabbed her key and stalked off.

'Whew!' Christy breathed. 'What's wrong with Her Highness? I thought you two were going to come to blows.'

'She was warning me away from Brad,' Sara exploded. 'He needs a "real" woman, not a "country girl in hiking boots"!' Her voice cracked.

Christy hooted. 'Hiking books! I think Ces finally went too far. Are you going to lie down and take it?' she asked curiously.

Sara stared at her sister a moment, then she grinned mischievously. 'No, no, I'm not.'

Hours later Sara happily surveyed herself in the hotel room mirror. Refusing to divulge her plans to Christy, she had only arranged to meet her at dinner with the others. In her hotel room she had hauled out the simple white dress she had brought as adequate for dining out, and instantly rejected it. Grabbing up her handbag, she had headed for the downtown area's most exclusive shops. Even now her conscience pinched at the exorbitant amount of money that she had spent that day.

'The results are worth it, the results are worth it,' she kept repeating out loud as she twirled in front of the mirror.

At the beauty salon, she had insisted that she must look gorgeous tonight, and hang the expense. The owner had looked keenly at her and then walked around her slowly, firing questions. He had called his assistant, they had mumbled together, then quickly swept Sara off to the back rooms. The results were all that she had demanded.

Her hair had been swept up on her head in a careless Gibson Girl knot which took two hours to achieve. Tendrils were allowed to curl over her forehead, in front of her ears, and at the nape of her neck. Only Sara and her hairdresser knew that the curls had been cunningly placed so that the effect was one of charming disarray. 'A soft look, as though a man's hands have already caressed you and will return again,' the hairdresser, surprisingly poetic, had said. Sara had been instructed how to apply her make-up to enhance this soft, feminine look.

As for her dress . . . she caught her breath as she looked in the mirror. Never had she paid so much for one outfit. But never, never had she had a dress this sensational. Waves of hand-painted colour shimmered on the fabric from midnight blue at the top through turquoise and greens, only to explode into a riot of pinks, fuchsias and scarlets forming a flowered border above the drifting hemline. Spaghetti straps held up a skimpy bodice which dipped to a deep sensuous vee, exposing the shadowy cleft between Sara's breasts. The simply cut dress closely followed the curves of her body before flaring dramatically out at her hips into a full circle. She walked across the room, loving the sound and the feel of the whispering silk chiffon swirling around her ankles in a cloud of colour.

Returning to the mirror, she needlessly rechecked her make-up and flicked here and there at her curls. Coward, she jeered in the mirror. Afraid you can't live up to a dress this sexy? She surveyed herself again. The dress was practically indecent. Should she change to the practical but modest white dress? She giggled as she speculated about everyone's reaction to this spectacular dress. Then she remembered Ces's derogatory remarks about hiking boots, and her resolution firmed up. This dress would let Ces know that Sara was a woman to be reckoned with! And, just maybe, Brad would see Sara as more than someone's kid sister. She wanted to see a glint in Brad's eye, and of a certainty, that old white rag wouldn't put it there.

Determined now, she picked up the dress's matching wrap and shrugged into it. Of midnight blue quilted silk chiffon, the coat buttoned securely from chin to hem, giving no hint of the flamboyant dress beneath.

Descending the Oriental rug-clad stairs down one floor to the lobby, Sara paused to look up at the ceiling. The lovely stained glass dome glowed with elegance, a fitting crown to the magnificent lobby. She always felt very wealthy staying in this beautifully appointed old hotel.

The others were all gathered in one corner waiting for her. As she walked over to them, Josh said impatiently, 'Hurry up. I'm hungry, and you've seen all this before.'

'That doesn't mean I can't still appreciate it,' Sara retorted.

'Your hair is charming,' Christy enthused. 'Is that where you disappeared to this afternoon?'

Sara nodded.

'A new dress, too, isn't it?' Christy asked.

This time Sara noticed the enthusiasm was missing from her sister's voice. In fact, a look almost of disappointment was on her face. Sara watched as her sister tried to unobtrusively compare Ces's outfit to Sara's. Ces was wearing an elegant creamy white polyester crêpe long shirtwaister, that made Sara glad she wasn't wearing her white dress. A heavy barbaric-looking necklace of silver and green malachite matched long dangling earrings. Sara could read Christy's mind that the severely cut blue coat of Sara's looked dowdy against Ces's sophistication. Christy herself looked sweet and virginal in a pale blue dotted Swiss peasant style dress. Sara had barely time to murmur her compliments on the dress to Christy when Brad was introducing the stranger who was standing beside him.

'Sara, this is Joe Roberts. Mr Roberts is my publisher and has consented to join us this evening.'

'The pleasure is all mine,' Grey eyes twinkled as the kindly-looking man shook Sara's hand gently. 'Let's go in and dine, shall we?' he said as he graciously offered her his arm.

Sara was grateful for Mr Roberts' astuteness. Evidently in the few moments of waiting in the lobby, he had come to the conclusion that Sara was the only unattached female in the party.

They entered the hotel dining room and followed the maitre d'hotel to a table in the corner away from the dance floor. Sara accepted the publisher's aid in removing her coat, and as she turned to thank him, she noted his look of appreciation. She heard Josh gasp in apparent shock and resolutely avoided Christy's eyes. Ces's looked as if she were mentally calculating the cost of the dress. There was no emotion on Brad's face at all when she finally dared peep at him from beneath lowered lashes.

'Have you any more surprises, Miss Blanchard?' Mr Roberts asked in a soft voice.

'Call me Sara,' Sara replied automatically. 'What do you mean?'

'Okay, Sara. And you call me Joe.'

Sara nodded her assent.

He indicated her coat. 'That promised one thing, but the dress tells a whole different story. I wish I'd had a camera to record all the different expressions around this table when they saw you.' He added shrewdly. 'I have a feeling you just stepped out of character, Sara.'

She blushed. 'I have a feeling you're right.'

'I think this evening is going to be even more entertaining than I'd anticipated.' He took a sip of wine and then turned back to her. 'Which one is your target?'

'What do you mean?' she stalled,

'You're dressed fit to kill. The question is, who's the victim?'

Sara gasped. 'Is it that obvious?'

Joe Roberts chuckled. 'I'm married and have four daughters about your age, so I guess you could say I have some experience.' He paused, but she ignored his earlier question. 'I understand this pretty young lady on my left is your sister, and I don't think you're the type to try and ambush your sister's boy-friend.'

'Ces is my cousin,' Sara said obliquely.

He understood the drift of her thoughts. 'Well, cousins aren't as close as sisters, are they? Besides, Ces looks fully qualified to protect her own property.'

'True,' Sara agreed glumly.

'Aha! So it is Brad,' the publisher said gleefully.

Fearfully Sara glanced around to see if anyone else was listening to this alarming conversation.

Mr Roberts laughed. 'Don't worry, Sara. They're all engrossed in their own conversations. I won't give your show away. Although, in all honesty, the other ladies at least suspect what's going on.'

'You think so?' Sara was horrified.

'Sure to. They think like women, too, you know.'

'Do you think . . . what about?' she couldn't put into the words the question she wanted answered.

'What about them?' The publisher indicated Josh and Brad.

'Yes.'

'I expect Mr Randall has been cued in on what's happening by your sister. He keeps giving you curious looks. As for Brad—well, when I helped you off with your coat, his jaw about fell off. Since then, who can tell? He hides his feelings very well.'

'I know,' Sara agreed dejectedly.

In an evident attempt to cheer her up, the publisher changed the channels of the conversation and soon had her laughing gaily at his accounts of his own daughters' rocky courtships. Now and again Sara glanced around the table and noticed that Josh and Christy were absorbed by one another as usual. Brad was steadily eating with occasional comments to Ces, who sat sullenly picking at her food. A little devil inside her told her gleefully that Ces didn't like being upstaged by Sara. Also she recalled Ces saying on the way to Denver that she wanted to talk with the publisher about writing a book on the modelling profession. When they had arrived at the table, Brad had pulled out a seat for Ces at the opposite end of the table from the publisher. With Sara on Mr Robert's right, Josh had quickly placed Christy on the man's left. Ces had known Josh all her life, and she could not be bothered to talk with him. Brad occasionally looked irritated as if he wanted to speak to Sara, but she was monopolised by his guest, and the music prevented talking across the table anyway. Secretly Sara was exhilarated by Brad's increasingly annoyed looks, knowing that she and Joe appeared very chummy to the rest of the table. Even Christy was tossing uncomprehending glances her way. Sara wondered what they would say if she told them the topic under discussion was Mrs Roberts' meat loaf recipe. In spite of herself, she giggled.

Joe looked surprised. 'Do you think cheese on meat loaf is funny? I assure you, it's delicious.'

Sara coloured guiltily. 'Yes, I'm sure it is.'

The publisher raised his eyebrows quizzically. 'You weren't listening.'

'Yes—yes, I was,' she hurried to convince him.

'No,' he sighed, 'I don't blame you. I'm sitting by the prettiest girl in the room, and we're talking about food!'

They laughed together, and as if by a signal, all the heads at the table turned to look at them.

Sara hastily looked at her plate, feeling the warm flush creep up her neck.

'You look deliciously guilty,' the publisher whispered into her ear. She looked up to see Joe's grey eyes smiling gently at her.

'I think he's getting jealous,' he added.

Sara stole a glimpse at Brad. His face was black as a thundercloud, and Ces was openly sulking.

Joe nudged Sara's attention back to himself. 'I'm glad they don't fight duels any more.'

'Don't be silly,' Sara said as a small sprig of hope grew in her heart. Was Brad really jealous?

The strolling violinists had stopped some time ago, and the dance band had been tuning up, and now they swung into a nostalgic tune of the fifties. Brad made as if to rise, and suddenly nervous, Sara turned to Joe Roberts and suggested that they dance.

The publisher was a big man, but he was also a quick one. Nimbly he got to his feet and held Sara's chair as she arose. They passed Brad still standing at his place with a nonplussed look on his face.

Sara soon discovered Joe was an excellent dancer, and she was enjoying following his lead as he executed several tricky manoeuvres. Josh and Christy followed them to the small dance floor, as did Brad and Ces.

When the music stopped, Brad and Ces were standing by Sara and her partner as they ended with a flourish of fancy steps. Brad frowned and then asked coolly, 'Care to change partners?'

Before Sara could reply, Ces stepped eagerly up to the publisher, and he whirled her away, winking at Sara over her cousin's shoulder. Sara grinned.

'Are you going to dance, or stand here and count your conquests?' Brad asked furiously.

'I beg your pardon?'

'Don't be coy with me! I can see how you're flirting with Joe Roberts.'

'Flirting?' Sara asked in astonishment. 'Just because Joe is easy to talk to . . .'

'Oh, it's Joe already, is it? I don't suppose that he mentioned to you that he's married. And has a family,' he added bitterly.

She looked at him astounded.

Before she could assure him that she knew all about the publisher's family, Brad continued his grievances in a barely controlled voice. 'I feel it's my duty to watch over you as Peter would have done for any sister of mine.'

Thoroughly vexed, Sara lost all desire to convince him that Joe Roberts had no dishonourable intentions. 'What if he does have a wife? She's not here now. We're both over twenty-one, and what I do is no business of yours.'

With such provocation, she hoped Brad would explain exactly why he was annoyed. To her disappointment, he was quiet a minute, and then stiffly agreed. 'You're right. I apologise. I was out of line in trying to interfere in what's obviously your own business.'

Sara decided to nudge him a little. 'Even if I'm not your type, that doesn't mean I'm nobody's type.'

'I wouldn't have thought your taste ran to married men.'

She shrugged in what she hoped was a nonchalant manner. 'Not usually, but when that's all that's available ...' Her voice trailed away as she waited hopefully for Brad to offer himself as a substitute. To her chagrin, he said nothing, and they continued to dance in awkward silence.

At last she was in Brad's arms, but they were stiff with disapproval and disgust. She felt miserable. She longed to melt closer to him, but was certainly receiving no encouragement from him to do so. She was glad when the dance finally ended.

'What a face!' the publisher teased her as she regained her seat beside him. 'Don't tell me the boyfriend doesn't like poaching on his private reserves?'

Sara grimaced. 'He just read me a lecture on married men.'

Joe choked on his laughter. 'You're kidding! What did he say when you told him we were comparing recipes?'

'I didn't tell him,' she answered defiantly. 'If he's so ready to think the worst of me, let him. What do I care? There are lots of men in this world.'

'But not for you,' the publisher reminded her gently.

She sniffed. 'Let's talk about something else.'

'All right.' The publisher was agreeable. 'Let's talk about your work. Brad was telling me about your photography.'

Soon Sara found herself confiding in this kind man her hopes for doing freelance photography. He heard her out in silence, then offered a suggestion.

'Listen, Sara. A friend of mine is an agent. Fix up a portfolio of your work and send it to him and get a professional opinion. He knows which magazines use freelance work, and if you have what it takes, he can steer you in the right direction, maybe even get you a job or two.'

'Really?' Sara could hardly believe her ears.

'Really,' Joe confirmed. He dug in his wallet and pulled out a business card. 'I don't have his address on me, as I thought, so send your portfolio to me, and I'll see that he gets it. I'll send a note with it to instruct him to give it his best personal attention,' he smiled.

'Oh, Mr Roberts—Joe, I mean. I don't know what to say, how to say thank you ...' Sara attempted to stammer out her gratitude.

The publisher patted her hand. 'Don't thank me, Sara. Either you're good, or you aren't.'

The remainder of the evening passed rapidly for Sara. She was so thrilled at the possible opportunities opening before her that she was barely aware of the people and happenings around her. She danced once with Josh and was vaguely aware that he was lecturing her, and she openly laughed at him to his vexation. Brad danced once again with her, but it was obvious he was still annoyed with her, and a little imp of mischief in her refused to let her set him straight.

It was growing late when Brad abruptly stood up and said he thought it was time to break up the party as they were making an early start the next day. Everyone obligingly arose.

The publisher touched Sara's arm. 'Would you care to join me for a nightcap?' He pointed to the cocktail lounge near the lobby. His words invited the whole table, but his glance invited Sara.

Sara was beginning to feel exhausted after the long day. 'Thank you, but no,' she declined regretfully, holding out her hand. 'It's been lovely meeting you, and thanks so much,' she added softly.

'Goodnight, lovely Sara. Be sure and send me that portfolio.'

During this interchange, everyone else had been gathering their coats. Brad picked up Sara's and held it for her. 'Why aren't you having a drink with him?' he asked quietly.

'Too tired,' Sara said.

Brad settled the coat over her shoulders, and she felt a light touch on her neck. Startled, she turned to see Brad's face close to hers. 'You wouldn't think they had flies in a snazzy joint like this, would you?' he asked in a light voice.

'Brad,' she said breathlessly, 'have you put me back among the human race?' Her neck tingled where his lips had touched.

'I don't know what you mean,' he said as he pressed her imperiously towards the exit.

'Well,' she said indignantly, 'you needn't push! Maybe I wasn't through telling everyone goodnight.'

'You'll see everyone but Joe Roberts tomorrow, and it seems to me the two of you must have thoroughly covered every subject in the world already this evening. If you were trying to irritate Ces by monopolising my publisher, you certainly succeeded.'

'Was Ces annoyed?' Sara asked sweetly.

Brad snorted. 'She was livid, and you know it. And who can blame her, when you made such a blatant pitch for the poor man?'

Sara stopped stock still. '*I* made a pitch? Did it ever occur to you that maybe he was doing the pitching? Just because you find me so undesirable, you needn't think everyone else does!'

'I don't know why you're so hung up on this idea that I don't find you desirable. Here,' he thrust out his hand.

She looked at him blankly. 'Here what?'

'We're at your room,' Brad said impatiently. 'Give me your key.'

Sara began to fumble in her jampacked purse. With a muttered curse, Brad grabbed it from her and groped around for the key. As he pulled it out, a white card fluttered to the carpeted floor. Before Sara could reach down, Brad stomped his foot on the card and then, unlocking the door, pushed Sara inside while he retrieved the card. It was Joe Roberts' business card.

'Well, well,' he said in a soft menacing voice as he

entered the room and shut the door behind him. 'What have we here?'

Playing for time, Sara held out her hand. 'Let me see it.'

Brad quickly moved the card out of her reach. 'You know what it is—Joe Roberts' card. I suppose this means you plan to carry on from tonight.'

'Carry on what?' she asked in exasperation.

He eyed her through narrow slits. 'I think I'll stay a while.'

'Why?'

'In case you're bothered by a late visitor.'

'Honestly, Brad, what a suspicious mind you have! I'm not expecting any visitors.'

'We'll see.'

Sara stamped her foot. 'Go away! I want to go to bed.'

Brad ignored her and walked over to the room's only chair and sat down. 'Go ahead.'

She stared incredulously at him. 'How can I, with you sitting here? You certainly have a strange idea of my morals! How can I convince you that no one is coming here, and that the only person bothering me is you?'

'Thirty minutes. If no one shows up in thirty minutes, I'll leave.'

'Leave now!' Sara cried, on the verge of angry tears. 'No one is coming, and if anyone were, it's not your business.'

'Your father expects me to look out after you.'

There was a knock on the door. Horrified, Sara stared at Brad. 'It must be Christy,' she whispered hoarsely.

Brad walked over and jerked open the door. Joe Roberts stood there. Sara moaned in dismay.

'Looking for someone?' Brad asked tersely.

'Yes, you. Randall said he thought he saw you come in here. Sorry to interrupt, but I just wanted to check what time we're getting together in the morning.'

'Eight-thirty in the coffee shop,' Brad answered in a frigid voice.

'Okay. 'Night. Goodnight, Sara,' the publisher called as he ambled away.

Shaky with relief, Sara collapsed against the wall as Brad closed the door. He turned a furious face to her, and she blanched. 'What's the matter now?'

'You don't really expect me to believe he was looking for me?' Brad jeered. 'The man certainly thinks fast!'

'Why, you——' Sara's hand shot out.

Before she could slap him, however, he had caught her arm. 'I apologise for ruining your evening,' he said coldly. 'Perhaps I can make it up to you.' His dark hooded eyes arrogantly roamed up and down the length of her body.

Sara guessed his intent, but moved back too late. One arm snaked around her waist and jerked her up hard against his muscular body. His other hand grasped the back of her head and forced her face to his. 'No!' she breathed, and then his lips were pressing on hers. She could feel her teeth cutting into her gums, and her lips felt numb. Shock kept her from breathing, and she began to feel faint. As if he realised, Brad released her lips, and she opened her mouth to gasp for air. Instantly he took advantage, again he invaded her mouth and demanded a response.

Vague yearnings propelled her movements. Her arms crawled up Brad's chest and clenched themselves behind his neck. One hand raked through his hair, and the other caressed his neck. She didn't think it possible, but he pulled her closer, and she could feel the rapid pulsating of his heart. Then his mouth left hers, and she felt forsaken and tried to turn her head to recapture his lips, but they were searing a path below her ear down to her neck, and she could feel her pulse beating frantically against his mouth. Weakly she leaned her head back against his shoulder and breathed deeply. The scent of shaving lotion mingled with after-dinner brandy wafted its sensuous way to her nostrils.

'There wasn't a man in that dining room tonight who could keep his eyes off you in that dress.' The husky words punctuated the light kisses Brad was raining on her neck and shoulders.

New delicious sensations coursed through her as he slipped the dress straps from her shoulders. Instinctively she moved in his arms to make her breasts more accessible to his searching hands. She moaned with delight as his hand smoothed slowly over one breast, and then his fingers began gently to fondle her nipple. Delectable feelings crawled deep down into her stomach region, then began building towards an unfamiliar, but exciting, crescendo.

Sara opened her eyes to see Brad watching her, a question in his eyes. She reached up and pulled his face down to hers so that their lips could mingle. As if her actions were a signal, his hand left her waist and grasping her hip, firmly ground it against his hard aggressive male body. Deep in her throat triumphant laughter gurgled, and she responded with a passion she had never dreamed she was capable of.

She felt the tingle of the zipper down the back, then her dress slowly slithered down her body with a silken whisper to lie in a forgotten heap on the floor. With a groan, Brad gathered her up and gently carried her over to the bed. She shifted to make room for him and eagerly lifted up her arms in welcome.

A sharp rap sounded on the door. Sara froze, but couldn't utter a sound. The knock was repeated.

'Who . . . who . . . is it?' she stammered at last.

'It's me, Ces,' her cousin's voice answered.

'What . . . what do you want?' Sara was sure Ces could hear her heart pounding clear out in the hallway.

'Where's Brad?' Ces asked.

'Why . . . why ask . . . me?' Sara managed to croak.

'Because I told him to get you away from Joe so I could talk to him,' Ces answered in an impatient voice. 'Then Brad was to meet me back at the cocktail lounge for a drink. He didn't show up, so I'm looking for him.'

Sara thought wildly, it's happening again. Once more, I'm just a diversion. Something to do to pass time. How could I delude myself into thinking that Brad really cared? She refused to look at him. 'I expect you just missed him. He's probably searching for you now. Why don't you go back to the lounge and wait? I'm sure whatever he's doing isn't important enough to keep him away from you for very long,' she added bitterly.

'You're right. I'll go back and see if he's there yet.'

Sara listened to Ces's footsteps lightly tapping down the hallway until the sound disappeared. In the room, there was silence, and still Sara refused to look at Brad. She pulled the sheet over her body and tried not to tremble as waves of shame and anger cascaded over her.

Finally Brad spoke in an emotionless voice. 'I see I've been judged, found guilty and hanged.'

Sara studied the wall with intense concentration. She was afraid she would burst into tears if she spoke. Let Brad convince her that he was not trying to deceive her again with his kisses. Why didn't he argue, smother her with kisses, persuade her to let him stay, convince her that he cared for her? Why should he? Ces was waiting for him now.

He stood by the bed looking at her. Bending down, he captured her chin with his hand and forced her to face him. 'I'm talking to you, Sara,' he muttered between clenched teeth.

His angry tone stabbed at Sara's heart. 'Don't touch me!' she cried out. 'I hate you!'

'I see.' He dropped her chin as if it were a hot coal. He turned his back to her and headed for the door. With his hand on the knob, he spoke once more. 'You still can't forgive me for living while Peter is dead, can you? Every time you see my scarred face, it must remind you of the past.' He paused. 'I'm about finished with my book, and then I'll be leaving the Valley. Until then, I'll take good care to stay out of your way.

Goodnight, Sara.' He added sardonically, 'Pleasant dreams.'

The door had barely clicked locked behind him before Sara dissolved in a torrent of tears. She wanted to die. Once again he had lifted her to the heights, only to callously dash her down again. How many times did he have to demonstrate how little she meant to him before she learned? What a fool she was!

This episode had shown her something else. She could never accept Roger's proposal. How could she possibly marry him, loving Brad as she did? Roger deserved better than the lukewarm love and friendship that was all she had to offer him. The bleak future stretched endlessly before her, and her weeping did nothing to relieve her grief and loneliness. Dawn was on the horizon when she finally fell into a restless, exhausted slumber.

CHAPTER EIGHT

SARA paused in surprise outside Ces's bedroom door. Suitcases were open everywhere, and clothes were strewn helter-skelter. Astonished, she stepped inside the room. They had returned from Denver the previous day, and Sara had not heard that Ces was making any plans to leave the Valley.

Ces turned from folding some slacks. 'Come to wish me a pleasant journey?'

The stiffening left Sara's knees, and she dropped to a chair. 'I . . . I didn't know you were leaving.' Was Brad going, too?

'Yes.' Ces folded a few more items of clothing. 'I called Sam this morning, and he misses me so, the poor darling, and begged me to come back. I'm feeling better, so . . .' She gave an elegant shrug.

'But . . . but . . . what about Brad?' asked Sara, dumbfounded.

'Oh, Brad,' said Ces in a disparaging tone. 'Brad was a pleasant diversion, that's all.'

'I thought that you and he . . . that he and you . . .' Sara foundered on the words.

Ces emitted a high artificial laugh. 'Really, Sara, can you see me as a military wife, faithfully trotting around after her husband? Of course, Brad is a dear boy and all that, and with enough money, I could even tolerate his scarred face. I wouldn't mind being the wife of a wealthy author, and the scars might then have a certain romantic appeal. But as it is,' she made a distasteful moue, 'I told him I just couldn't see myself giving up everything for what little he has to offer, since he insists on staying in the Air Force.'

'Ces!' Sara squeaked in horror. 'Surely you didn't say that to him?'

162

'Sara, you're too tender-hearted,' said Ces, in a patronising tone. 'Brad is more realistic. He knows only his wealth would make his appearance acceptable to me. Do you think I want people feeling sorry for me because Brad is the best I could do?'

Sara was nauseated. 'Ces,' she said in a barely controlled voice, 'I feel sorry for you now. You can't measure a man of Brad's worth by his bank account or his looks. You've made a dreadful mistake.'

'Darling,' Ces snapped her last suitcase closed, 'if you think he's such a bargain, you may have him with my blessing.'

Her mind ripped asunder by Ces's callous remarks, Sara numbly left the room. If only he wanted me, she thought. If only he wanted me! Tears streamed down her face as she remembered Brad talking about his return from Vietnam and his wish that he had been loved. He had loved Ces, and she had cruelly rejected him, jeering at his honourable wounds. Ces wasn't worth his little finger. Sara wished she could feel jubilant that Brad was faced with bitter rejection, just as he had rejected her. But, loving him, his pain became hers, and she cried for the hurt that Ces had cruelly and thoughtlessly inflicted.

Josh and Christy volunteered to drive Ces to Aspen to catch a plane, and she left after lunch with much fanfare. Sara had barely endured the meal. Brad's face failed to give any hint of his feelings about Ces's departure.

The evening that Ces left, Sara and her father dined alone. Brad had remained in his cabin to work, and Christy had not returned yet from Aspen. After dinner, Sara challenged her father to a game of chess. For some time they played quietly before the fire, concentrating on the demands of the game.

The Judge took a sip of coffee and then spoke, carefully studying the chessboard. 'Brad was by today.'

'Yes, I saw him at lunch, remember?'

'Oh, yes—well, this was later in the afternoon. He had some news.'

'What news?'

'The book is done.' The Judge closely scrutinised his fingernails. 'He's leaving tomorrow.'

'Leaving?' Sara felt as if she had been unexpectedly punched in the stomach. 'But . . . he can't . . . that is, his time isn't up . . . I mean . . . I thought he still had another month's vacation.'

The Judge shrugged. 'I guess everything just fell into place, and now he's finished with the book and anxious to leave.'

Sara seemed to have trouble breathing.

'That news should make you happy.' Her father watched her closely.

'Me?' Sara cried.

'You never did like it that I asked Brad here while you were here. I'm sorry he spoiled your vacation.'

'He didn't exactly spoil it.'

'Well, he said to tell you goodbye, and now you'll have a week without tripping over him,' the Judge pointed out heartily.

'Yes,' Sara agreed. It was too sudden. She didn't want Brad to leave. She'd just been marking time hoping something, anything would happen to make Brad come to love her. If only he would see her as a woman, as well as Peter's sister! She dropped her coffee cup on to its saucer with a clatter. Standing up, the chess game forgotten, she started out of the room.

'Sara, before you go, I have to tell you something.'

The distress in her father's voice drew her back into the room. 'Daddy, what is it?'

'I am ashamed to tell you this, but I have a confession to make. Eight years ago I did a terrible thing, and what's worse, I forgot all about it until a few days ago. I hope you can forgive me for this, Sara . . .' her father's voice faltered.

She flew to his chair and hugged him fiercely.

He held her tight as he continued. 'Brad called for you.'

Sara was perplexed. 'What do you mean?'

'After he was released.'

'What?' Shock drove her upright.

Her father retained her hand. 'It must have been about a month after he was released. I told him you didn't want to talk to him.'

'What?' she recoiled.

'Sara, please,' her father pleaded. 'It sounds worse than it was. You were so upset about Peter, as we all were. I didn't know who Brad was, and I was afraid talking with a friend of Peter's would be too much of an ordeal for you.' His eyes watched her anxiously.

'What did you say to him?'

'I just told him you were too upset to speak with him. He seemed to understand.'

Sara could barely breathe. 'Why are you telling me this now?'

The Judge's face was filled with compassion. 'Since you've arrived, Sara, it's been obvious that there's some kind of undercurrent between you and Brad. I was at a loss to understand it because I thought you'd just met. It had to be more than the fact that Brad was Peter's friend. Even the fact of your correspondence didn't seem to account for it. Unless,' he looked shrewdly at Sara, 'unless there was more than mere friendship involved. Suddenly I remembered the phone call, and I asked Brad if it had been he who'd called—I'm sorry, Sara, I'd forgotten the name before I ever hung up the telephone.'

'What ... what did Brad ... say?' Sara could hardly speak.

'He acknowledged making the call, and I explained the circumstances and apologised to him. He passed it off lightly, but it seemed to me that there was lingering hurt. I tried to apologise again, but,' the Judge shrugged, 'how do you explain and apologise for interference, no matter how well intentioned, that may have changed a person's life eight years ago?'

Sara slowly withdrew her hand from her father's clasp.

'What are you going to do, Sara?' he enquired gently.

She turned glazed eyes in his direction. 'I don't know yet,' she admitted.

When her trembling legs had finally conveyed her to the sanctuary of her room, her thoughts exploded into chaos. She wanted to wail out her anger and distress for the wasted years. Bewildered, she sat and tried to organise her thoughts. Brad had tried to contact her. To discover after all these years that Brad had not rejected her, but rather that she had rejected him, no matter that she was ignorant of the fact, was a considerable shock. Brad had as much as said that day in her room that he had expected to see her when he'd got off the plane. And then, when he had called, her father had told him that she didn't want to speak to him. Surely that explained his feelings that Peter's death was a barrier?

Conflicting emotions raged through Sara's breast. She wanted to rush out and confront Brad with her discovery that he had called, to tell him that she loved him, but fear held her back. Brad knew she hadn't been told about the call. Why hadn't he mentioned it to Sara?

There still existed impediments. There was Ces. There were the hasty words with which Sara had lashed out at Brad. The anger, the frustrations, the rejection of the past years strangled her now in their coils of fear and indecision.

She forced herself to study the situation from Brad's viewpoint. He had been rejected too many times; he wouldn't come to her again. The next move was up to her.

Sara slowly rocked back and forth, her arms folded tightly together as if to warm her uncertain body. She loved Brad so much. Was she strong enough to put his needs before her pride?

What if Brad didn't love her, didn't want her? He had never written any words of love. Neither did you, Sara reminded herself. She had wanted to tell Brad in person. Later she had been happy that at least some small measure of pride had been salvaged.

Now she wasn't so sure. Maybe if she had told Brad that she loved him, he would have tried harder to reach her. She sighed, impatient with her thoughts of the past. The present was all that counted now.

It didn't matter if Brad loved her, did it? He had told her he desired her. She could go to him now and offer herself. She owed him that much. And would it be such a great sacrifice on her part? True, she risked heartbreak and rejection, but she had to try. She couldn't spend the rest of her life wondering about what might have been. Even if Brad didn't love her, she would have her one night of happiness, of fulfilment.

She stepped from the tub and slowly blotted her body dry. Apprehension slowed her motions, the coming scene vivid in her mind. Sitting down, she deftly applied a minimum of make-up. She dried her hair and then fluffed it to hang loose to her shoulders.

From the closet she pulled out clean clothing. In a hasty decision, underwear was flung to the floor, and she quickly shrugged on her jeans before she lost her courage. Next came a red silk shirt that Brad hadn't seen her in. The blouse clung to her skin, the sheer fabric enhancing the fullness of her breasts. She slipped a silver chain around her neck and stepped back to survey the results. The effect was right, subtle, yet obvious that a woman was beneath the clothing. She hesitated and then unbuttoned the blouse several buttons. Twisting sideways, she could see the dark shadow of cleavage. She dabbed perfume on her pulse spots, and blowing herself a kiss in the mirror for luck, slid her feet into moccasins and slipped out of the bedroom door. Halfway down the stairs she heard her father's voice.

'That you, Sara?'

'Yes, Dad,' she answered, hastily buttoning up her blouse.

'Is everything okay?'

'Yes, I . . . I think I'll take a short walk.'

'All right. Tell Brad to stop by in the morning before he leaves.'

Sara was momentarily silenced. 'What makes you think I'll see Brad?' she asked at last.

Her father only chuckled.

Sara thought her face probably matched her red shirt as she went out of the door. She paused to try and regain her composure. Looking down at her blouse, she resolutely unbuttoned it again. Then, taking her courage in both hands, she started around the yard to Brad's cabin.

The lights were on in the cabin, and the shades not yet drawn. Sara could see Brad walking back and forth across the room. She wondered again if she were crazy, throwing herself at him like this. What if he laughed at her, or worse yet, felt sorry for her? In spite of herself, her steps slowed, and her fingers fumbled to fasten her shirt together again. Sara, you're being ridiculous, she admonished herself, and forced her legs to climb the two steps to Brad's door. Hesitantly she rapped on the door. Looking down, she unbuttoned her blouse once more.

Brad flung open the screen door. 'Sara! To what do I owe the honour of your visiting me?' He glanced at her blouse front, and she would have sworn that in that instant he divined her plan. He opened the door wider. 'Come in.'

Sara held herself tautly as she went into the guest cabin. Striving for composure, she glanced around the single room. Made of pale yellow peeled pine logs, the walls rose to a high peak in the middle while huge beams ran from wall to wall supporting the ceiling. A back door led to a glassed-in sun-porch, while one corner of the square room had been partitioned off to provide a small bathroom cubicle. A native stone fireplace dominated the end wall, and this evening a cosy fire burned, throwing shadows on the facing sofa. Framed photographs hung above the mantel, and she didn't need to walk closer to know that they were her work. The furniture was covered in serviceable browns and beiges, but a red striped afghan across the sofa back and a motley assortment of patchwork pillows added bright dashes of colour. A day bed at one side was covered with a red checked throwover, and on this Sara saw Brad's suitcase open as if she had interrupted him in the act of packing.

'Did you come merely to check out the cabin?' Brad asked in a derisive tone. 'Maybe I could offer you a beer while you count the silver to see if any is missing.'

Sara's small amount of courage was fast fleeing. 'A beer would be nice,' she said as she sat down on the sofa.

Brad moved across the cabin to the kitchen area. Bright yellow open wooden cupboards on either side of the sink held chipped and cast off dishes. An electric hotplate and an electric skillet provided the only means of cooking. As Brad poured the beer, Sara noticed that the red-topped chrome kitchen table was loaded with a typewriter, mounds of papers and other evidences of his writing. Other piles of papers were stacked neaby on the floor. She frowned. Surely that was where the double bed had stood? She looked about again, but there was no sign of the bed. It must have been removed at some time, and Brad must use the day bed.

He came back and handed her a beer with the foam threatening to run down the side of the glass. She carefully concentrated on the amber bubbles as he joined her on the sofa.

'This is the first time you've come over here. What's the special occasion?'

Sara continued to show great interest in her beer. 'I thought I'd come and say goodbye.'

'Goodbye!' Brad exclaimed. 'Are you going somewhere?'

She flashed him an irritated look. 'I know you're leaving in the morning.'

'I'm leaving in the morning?' he echoed. 'Where did you hear that?'

'Dad told me.' Sara added carefully, 'He didn't say why.'

'He didn't,' Brad mused. 'What did he say?'

Sara shrugged. 'Not much. Just that you'd finished up your manuscript and had no further reason to stay.'

'I see,' said Brad in a noncommittal voice.

She sipped her beer in a silence that seemed fraught with tension.

'I didn't know you liked beer,' Brad commented. 'You never wanted one while we were camping.'

Sara looked at her glass. 'I drink one occasionally.' She hated beer; it gave her headaches. She took another sip. 'This is very refreshing.'

Brad laughed and took the beer from her hand and sat it with his on the small chest that served as a table before the sofa. He sat studying her.

Sara thought her nerves would snap as the silence between them grew.

'So you came to say goodbye,' Brad finally observed.

'Yes,' she said.

'Being the dutiful hostess?'

'No.'

He quirked an eyebrow. 'You're a real conversational fireball tonight, aren't you?'

She shifted slightly on the sofa, turning to face him. She saw his eyes open wide as he glanced at the vee of her shirt. Without looking down she knew she must be exposing a great deal of skin. A nerve twitched in Brad's cheek, and Sara reached up and traced the small scar beneath his ear.

Swiftly he reached up and imprisoned her hand. 'What do you really want, Sara?' he drawled in a soft, ominous voice.

She thought wildly, it's now or never. She casually leaned one shoulder back in what she hoped was a provocative pose. 'Brad, I came to tell you goodbye,' she insisted.

'Goodbye,' he said coolly, and stood up.

Sara arose and slid her hands up his shirt front and grasped the lapels. 'I thought I'd kiss you goodbye,' she stated in a prim little voice.

'Did you?'

She raised up on tiptoe and lightly brushed her lips across Brad's. There was no response. She fastened her hands together behind his neck and tugged his head down. Using more firmness, she kissed him again. Brad remained unresponsive. Her tongue lightly flickered across his tightly closed lips and across his cheek. Boldly she nibbled on his ear and rained kisses down his scar.

He grabbed her hands and shoved her away from him. 'I don't think I care for your pity, Sara.'

'Pity?' she cried in disbelief.

'You already told me how you feel about my scars, and I saw you speculating when Ces left so suddenly. Let me ease your curiosity. Ces didn't like my scars any more than you do. She told me she felt her beauty deserved someone who better matched her own appearance.'

'Oh no!' appalled, Sara shook her head in dismay.

'Oh yes,' Brad mocked. 'At least Ces was honest with me. She didn't come over here feeling sorry for me and try to make it up to me.'

Sara was aghast. 'It's not like that at all!'

'Really, Sara? Really?' he asked contemptuously. 'I suppose you're half naked because the weather is so warm this evening.'

His scornful words exploded the careful curb she had been maintaining on her emotions. 'I'm not half naked,' she spat as she ripped off her shirt.

Brad stared in open-mouthed amazement.

Hastily Sara kicked off her moccasins, unzipped her jeans and stepped out of them as they fell to the floor. 'There—I'm not half naked. I'm totally naked!' she yelled. 'I came over here to seduce you, and I've never seduced a man before, and I don't know how to do it, and I'd like a little co-operation!' Her anger vanished in the face of Brad's total astonishment. 'Please,' she added in a quivering voice. 'I'm scared.'

His eyes flared. He grabbed her and pulled her to his chest and passionately, forcefully, kissed her mouth. 'Is that better?' he muttered.

'Umm. You talk too much,' she replied. She pressed her body closer.

He pushed her away, a cool level gaze searching her face. 'Are you sure this is what you want?'

'Yes, I am,' she answered steadily.

Swiftly Brad swung her up into his arms and turned towards the door leading to the sun-porch. On the sun porch was the double bed, and he gently placed her on it.

'I wondered where it was,' she murmured.

He paused in the act of unbuttoning his shirt. 'What?'

'The bed. I wondered where it was.'

He laid his long length beside Sara. 'I pushed it out here to watch the stars and see the rising sun.' He leaned down and brushed the hair from her face. 'Tonight you can watch the stars with me,' he promised in a thick voice.

'Later,' Sara agreed.

Then Brad's lips were on her own, demanding, taking, owning her mouth. Sensations rippled gently through her veins and then were faster and hotter until she thought she would drown in her desires. Having dominated her mouth to his satisfaction, Brad turned his attention to her ear-lobes, her neck, then she moaned with pleasure as his lips scattered kisses down to her breasts. She felt him gently kiss her healing wound before his lips captured her tautened nipples. She rolled under him to crush herself closer to his hard manliness, and his body pressed her into the mattress. He boldly claimed her entire being, and she gladly surrendered as he led her to the final ecstasy.

Sara woke up slowly. The morning sun caressed her

face, and she wondered why she had forgotten to close her bedroom curtains. Then Brad's even breathing sounded beside her, and the memories of last night flooded back. A tight band encircled her waist, and she realised that Brad still slept with his arm around her.

Her body felt languid, and she was content to lie still beside him, enjoying the touch of his silken skin the length of her. A warm flush crept over her flesh as she dwelt on the passion he had exhibited during the night, a sweet tender passion. He had been a patient lover, banking down his own urgent fires to ignite her slower passions, waiting until she was consumed with desire before he had led her to joyful fulfilment. Once during the night his gentle touch had awakened her to a sense of his needs, and she had been quick to respond.

Her first night of love had been beautiful and satisfying. Only one devilish imp now raised its mocking head. Brad had uttered many words of passion, but none of love. Making love and being in love were two sides of the same coin to Sara, but Brad could evidently separate his physical and emotional needs.

Carefully she turned her head to gaze at him. In repose, the pain etched lines were fainter, but still she had to fight the urge to reach over and cover his face with healing kisses. She loved him so much. How she longed for that love to be returned! Yet she had asked Brad for no commitments, and now she could not turn on him with recrimination for taking what she had freely offered.

His lips parted in his sleep, and Sara's body quivered responsively as she remembered how those same lips had transported her during the night, eliciting uninhibited response from her. Her lips quirked. One thing she felt certain of, Brad had enjoyed the night as much as she. He might not love her, but at least he was satisfied by her. No matter what happened now, no one could take her night of happiness away from her. As she watched him, Brad sighed and rolled over on his side, his back to her. Slowly she eased her way out of the bed.

Brad's dark brown terrycloth robe was tossed across a near-by chair, and she slipped it on. Fastening the belt securely around her waist, she tiptoed from the sun-porch into the main room of the cabin. She filled the tea-kettle and put it on the electric hot plate to boil. Searching through the cupboards, she discovered instant coffee and two mugs. She waited impatiently for the water to boil, then fixed herself a cup of coffee. Curling her fingers around the mug to ward off the morning's chill, she debated whether to rouse Brad. Finally she decided to shower first. Closing the bathroom cubicle door behind her, she hoped the sound of the running water wouldn't wake him. Using Brad's shower, his soap and his towels gave her a vicarious pleasure.

After her shower, she wrapped herself in his robe again, having neglected to collect her own clothing. She padded on bare feet to the sun-porch doorway. Brad lay face down, arms flung wide, still soundly sleeping. Sara blew him a kiss and then padded silently back to the kitchen area. Quietly she gathered food from the refrigerator, cracked eggs, sliced sausage links and chopped onion and cheese into the electric skillet. In minutes an omelette was bubbling merrily in browned butter, sending savoury smells wafting into the air. Sara smiled as she heard bed-springs creaking on the porch. Brad was waking at last. Her eyes spied a battered tray on the cupboard top, and she hauled it down and loaded it with small glasses of the orange juice she had discovered in the refrigerator, as well as napkins and cutlery. Next, steaming hot mugs of coffee went on the tray. Finally the piping hot omelette was rolled into delectable piles on plates and added to the tray. Picking up the heavy load, Sara carried it to the sun-porch.

'Good morning,' she said brightly as she placed the tray on a table beside the bed. 'Hungry?'

'Yes, but I suppose I'll have to eat this first, since you went to so much trouble.'

Sara blushed as the meaning of his words sunk in. 'Not so much trouble.' She ignored his other words.

Brad grinned. 'My robe looks better on you than me.'

'Thank you.' She handed him his coffee as he propped himself up to a sitting position. She averted her eyes from his bare chest. The scars didn't bother her. Rather, she wanted to ignore breakfast and crawl in next to him, running her hands up his chest, tug lightly on his crinkly chest hairs, and press her body next to his, to feel and hear their hearts beat as one.

Brad raised an eyebrow as if he could read her thoughts, and smiled at her. 'After breakfast,' he promised.

Embarrassed, Sara changed the subject. 'How are your eggs?'

'Delicious.' He toasted her with his coffee mug. 'Having a live-in maid is the only way to go.'

'We'll rotate,' Sara retorted. 'Tomorrow I get breakfast in bed.' Appalled at the words that had slipped out, she took a hasty gulp of coffee and choked on it.

'Okay?' Brad asked in concern.

'Yes. Just eat your breakfast,' she ordered.

'Ah, in a hurry, are you?'

Sara blushed again. Would her unwary tongue never be still?'

He handed her his empty plate and mug and then patted the bed beside him. 'Come here,' he directed.

Suddenly shy, she puttered with the dirty dishes, stacking and unstacking them on the tray.

'Sara——' Brad reached out a hand to grab her wrist and tugged her towards him.

She sat down on the edge of the bed. Nervously she looked out the window, anywhere but at Brad.

He ran his fingers lightly up and down her arm. Even through the heavy fabric of the robe, the light touch sent dancing tremors through her body. 'Are you sorry about last night?' he asked.

'Sorry?' She couldn't tell him her only sorrow was that he didn't love her.

He shrugged. 'I know it was your first time. I wouldn't want you to be feeling guilty or besmirched this morning.'

Involuntarily Sara chortled. 'I wouldn't exactly say I feel besmirched . . .' she began.

He eyed her closely. 'How do you feel about last night, Sara?'

'Smug,' she said defiantly.

The solemness left Brad's face, to be replaced with comic surprise. 'Smug?' he repeated.

'Smug,' Sara reiterated firmly. 'You're right, it was my first time, and I thought I acquitted myself pretty good. I did, didn't I?'

Brad's eyes laughed, but he answered gravely enough. 'Yes, you acquitted yourself very good.'

'Only one thing . . .' Sara was facing him now, her finger tracing patterns on his chest. Her eyes refused to rise higher than his chin.

'One thing?' Brad prompted.

'I think I need more practice,' she blurted.

He laughed out loud and drew her to him. 'Is that something I can help you with?' he muttered into her hair.

'Please,' Sara requested demurely.

Then his possessive hands were on her, demanding that she surrender her mind and her body to their mutual passion.

Surfeited, Sara dozed. Vaguely aware of Brad leaving her side, she moaned in disappointment. He chuckled, and she felt a light kiss on her cheek, then the covers were tucked around her, and she slept.

'Sara, wake up!' Brad's voice tugged her up from sleep. She resisted, pulling the blankets up over her head. 'What a lazybones!' Laughter lurked in his voice, and then he swept the covers from her, and the cold air awakened her instantly.

'You meanie!' she stormed. 'Give me back my blankets—I'm cold!'

'No wonder,' he leered suggestively.

Sara looked down at her naked body and was abashed.

'You're beautiful, Sara,' Brad said softly, and then taking pity on her embarrassment, he tossed her his robe.

She snuggled up warmly, then properly viewed Brad for the first time since he had awakened her. He was wearing his blue Air Force uniform. Handsome in any clothes, the uniform enhanced his looks, accentuated his military bearing, and emphasised his masculinity. 'How nice you look,' Sara said inadequately.

He sketched her a mock salute. 'Thank you, ma'am.'

She let her eyes feast on him. How sexy men looked in uniform! The armed forces would be overcrowded if men realised the impact a man in uniform could have on a woman's heart, she thought. Suddenly the implications of Brad's wearing his uniform cut through her other thoughts like a keen-edged blade. Last night didn't count with him; he was still leaving this morning. Her heart sank to her toes, and she knew her face must reflect her thoughts.

Brad's face stilled as he looked at her. 'Silly goose,' he said softly.

'I . . . I don't know what . . . what you mean,' Sara stuttered, determined not to cry.

'I mean that you took one look at my uniform and jumped to a lot of conclusions.'

She held her back stiff. 'You're free to do as you please.' She blindly stuck out her hand in Brad's general direction. 'Goodbye.'

He hooted with laughter.

The sound dried the threatened tears from Sara's eyes, and she glared at him with hostility. 'What's so funny?'

Brad gathered her unresponsive body up off the bed and hugged her tight. 'You're funny,' he said. 'Now hurry up and get dressed or you'll make us miss our plane.' He shoved her towards the main room, adding a swat on her bottom.

'Us?' Sara was stunned.

'Us,' he affirmed. 'You certainly didn't think I would leave you after last night, did you? Besides,' he added in a teasing voice, 'you still need practice.'

'But ... I can't just up and leave ... I can't ... what about my clothes ... my vacation ... what about Dad ...? The questions tumbled out, leaving her breathless.

Brad centred in on the most pertinent question. 'I talked to your dad this morning, and Christy brought over some clothes for you.' He handed Sara her denim wrap skirt, a blue and white striped oxford shirt and underwear. 'I hope that's all you need. Christy packed a small case with make-up and other essentials she thought you'd want.'

'You talked to my dad ... a make-up case ... Brad, I don't understand what's going on here.'

'You dress, I'll talk,' Brad directed.

Sara hastily shrugged into her clothes and then worked on her face as he lounged against the bathrom door watching her.

'I think your father was playing matchmaker,' he told her.

'What?' Sara rubbed off the black line where she'd smeared her mascara in her surprise.

'He seems to have deliberately misled you. I had planned to go up to Denver for the day only. I would have been back this evening. That fact was very clear to your father.'

'What?' Once again, Sara had to repair mascara damage.

'I'm going up to Denver to have my picture taken for the book jacket—that's why I'm wearing my uniform. When I talked to your dad yesterday I told him I'd miss dinner here, but be back late tonight.'

Sara turned on him. 'Why, you ... you ...' Indignantly she waved her mascara brush at him. 'You let me . . . you let me . . . I thought . . .' she spluttered in her fury.

Brad laughingly held her hands so her mascara didn't stain his uniform. 'I'm afraid I'm guilty there,' he admitted. 'It seemed a shame to waste that performance you were bound to give.'

'Why, you . . . you . . . I'll . . . I'll . . .!' Sara couldn't think of any threat potent enough. 'I think I'll stay here. You don't need me along today anyway. I'd just be in your way,' she pouted.

'We both have to be there to sign for a marriage licence.'

'Marriage licence?'

'It's generally considered necessary when two people plan to get married.'

'Married?' she gasped.

Brad said smoothly, 'Of course you and I are getting married.'

'Married?' Sara felt idiotic repeating his words. She clutched the rim of the sink to steady herself. 'I don't remember any talk of marriage,' she managed at last.

'Did I neglect to mention that?' Brad asked.

'Yes, you did,' she said bluntly. 'Why do you bring it up now?'

'I rather thought after last night and this morning it would be understood.'

'Did you? Why?' She applied lipstick with shaking hands. She loved Brad, but she couldn't marry him unless he loved her.

'When a man sleeps with a woman in her father's house . . .' Brad's voice died away.

Suddenly a horrible suspicion struck her. Did Brad think she'd seduced him deliberately to force him to ask her to marry him? Fiercely she turned on him. 'No, I won't marry you! I don't want to marry you!'

He looked thunderstruck. Then he tried reasoning with her. 'Surely after last night—I mean, your father expects—that is, I told him we were getting married.'

'Well, you can just un-tell him!' Sara noticed Brad

didn't mention love. 'I wouldn't marry you if you were the last man on earth!'

His face went cold and bleak. 'Of course,' he said distantly, 'how stupid of me. I thought you came to me last night because you loved me. I was forgetting about the scars. They make you sick, don't they? A fling here where no one sees us is one thing. It was naïve of me to forget women have physical needs to be met, too. I suppose in the dark, that was more important than my scars, but daylight is a whole different story. You can't bear to be seen with me in public.' He turned to go. 'I'll remove my offensive face at once. Perhaps someone will pack up my things and send them on. Your father has my address. I hope you'll be very happy with your rich and handsome Roger.'

'Brad, no!' The words burst from Sara's lips, but Brad didn't even hesitate. Paralysed with shock, Sara couldn't move as he went out of the screen door and turned towards the garage.

Then she remembered that the garage was near the sun-porch, and she rushed to the window and threw it open. 'Brad, you come back here and listen to me!' she screamed. 'You always walk out on me when I try to explain! Yes, your scars make me sick, and yes, I hate to look at them. But it's not what you think. I get sick because when I see those scars, I remember what hell you've gone through. I hate to see them because I wasn't there to console you when you were in pain. It's a part of your life I can never share. I can never understand how you felt, and what you suffered. I see those scars on your face, and they remind me that you got off the plane and you were alone, and I hate myself for that. All I want to do when I see your scars is hold you and try to kiss away the hurt and pain. I hate everything those scars stand for. Do you hear me? I hate it, I hate it, I hate it! Are you listening?' She leaned as far into the window as the screen allowed and shrieked in the direction of the garage. 'Are you listening?' She strained but couldn't hear a car engine. 'Brad Rawlins, did you hear me?' she shouted again.

'The whole valley heard you.' The quiet words spoken behind Sara caused her to jump and hit her head on the window sash. The bump brought tears of pain to her eyes. Immediately concern darkened Brad's eyes, and he hurried to enfold her in his arms. 'Poor baby,' he soothed. 'I'm always causing you pain, it seems.'

Sara backed out of his arms. 'Where did you come from?' she demanded breathlessly. 'I thought ... I thought ... you'd ... you'd gone ...' Her voice caught.

'I started to leave,' Brad admitted. 'I was almost to the garage when I realised I didn't have the car keys. I came in the door just as you started yelling.' He smiled ruefully. 'Why didn't you tell me all this before?'

Sara concentrated on tracing his name on his uniform name tag with her finger. 'I tried once, and then ...' her voice fell.

'And then?' Brad prodded.

'There was Ces.'

'Ces?' His voice was puzzled. 'What does Ces have to do with anything?'

'She's so beautiful, and I thought you cared for her. She said you wanted to marry her.' Sara's voice grew fainter and fainter.

'Ces may be beautiful, but there's no warmth, no compassion there. She is also a liar. After I left you that night in your hotel room in Denver, Ces and I had it out between us. I hadn't told her I'd get you out of the way or that I'd meet her later. Joe Roberts let slip that I was in your room, and I'm afraid Ces is just a natural trouble-maker. I strongly convinced her that she'd be much happier away from the Valley.' He emphasised the word 'strongly'. 'I couldn't have her shooting any more of her poisonous darts at you. And I never wanted to marry her. She did indicate that if I decided to leave the service and make lots of money for her to spend, she'd be agreeable. But I never loved Ces. It would be like loving a beautiful porcelain statue.' He tipped up Sara's chin. 'I like a woman with warmth, humour and passion.' He kissed her nose. 'She has to share my love of the outdoors, make light of discomfort, have the courage to face and overcome obstacles.' His face lightened. 'However, it is not necessary that she can touch worms.'

Sara's heart turned over at the look in his eyes. Surely that was love! He's never said he loves you, an inner voice warned. Don't be stupid, a second voice countered—how lonely Brad has been, how much he has suffered, would he risk rejection again? As Sara's thoughts raced wildly around in her head, Brad had been waiting for her to end the silence. When she didn't do so, his face closed, his smile dimmed, and he turned away. The slump of his shoulders decided her. She'd have to gamble it now. 'I love you,' she forced the words out. 'That's why I came to you last night.'

Brad stopped short, paused and then pivoted on his heels. 'Say that again,' he demanded, a look of awe on his face.

'I love you, I love you, I love you,' Sara chanted, devouring with her eyes the look of rapture on his face.

'Oh Sara—oh Sara!' Brad whispered brokenly as he grabbed her shoulders. 'Sara, I love you so much.' The ringing tones sent thrills up her spine.

'You do?' she asked stupidly.

'I do,' he said positively as he pulled her close.

She drew back. 'Why didn't you say so?' she wailed, the frustrations of the past weeks sounding in her cry.

'I wanted to. At first I was vain enough to think you felt something for me, too. You kept shoving Roger between us. I thought you had made him up as a barrier against me. No one else seemed to know of his existence. That gave me hope, and there was no denying your response whenever I touched you. Then Roger called, and all my hopes crumbled. Last night when you came to me, I dared to dream again, but you never said you loved me. I worried that if I said I loved you, I'd look in your eyes and see pity.' His hands clutched her shoulders in remembered despair. 'I was so afraid.

Compared to Roger, what do I have to offer you, a scarred old wreck like me?' he asked bitterly.

Sara's lips reached up and nuzzled his scar. 'Love?' she suggested. 'You can give me love.'

Brad groaned and embraced her so tightly that she feared her ribs would crack. 'Love? Yes, I have so much love to give you, my adorable Sara. Since the first day I fell in love with a pigtailed, freckled-faced teenager, I've wanted to love and cherish you for the rest of my days.'

'You have?' she asked in amazement.

'I have,' he assented gravely. 'A picture of you sat on Pete's desk, and I was jealous of your brother. It irritated me the way he took your daily letters for granted. I don't mean Pete didn't love you,' he hastened to assure her.

'I know,' Sara said softly, 'I spoiled him, and he accepted that, but he still loved me.'

He gave her a quick hard kiss. 'I love you. Anyway, it bugged me more and more how cavalier Peter was with your affection, and I nagged him more and more to write to you more often. Finally in disgust he yelled at me to write to you myself. I think that secretly that was what I wanted all along. I loved your letters.' Sara received another quick kiss.

'You did?' she wrinkled her nose. 'They must have sounded so immature.'

'They were beautiful,' Brad insisted. 'In the beginning you wrote such prim and proper letters, but then you began opening like a rose. You laid your thoughts bare before me, and I was honoured to be so entrusted. It became clear that you thought of me in heroic terms, and I found myself wanting to live up to your ideals of courage and honesty. There were countless temptations, and many times a look at your picture or a phrase you had written served to set me back on the straight and narrow.'

'Oh, Brad!' Sara was thrilled to hear that she had inspired him.

He went on. 'Pretty soon I was aware my feelings

about you were not exactly brotherly, but I knew I couldn't say anything to you. You were so young.'

'Sixteen,' Sara interrupted.

'Sixteen, and I was twenty-three. At that age, seven years is quite a gap. I don't seem too old now?' he asked anxiously.

'You're just right,' she assured him, and kissed him lightly to encourage him.

He smiled his appreciation. 'I planned how I'd come home with Pete, and we'd get to really know each other.' He lapsed into a brooding silence.

Sara clutched him tight to help ease his pain. She could never make him forget that hell, but she hoped she was strong enough to help him overcome his memories. Silent tears ran down her face.

Her tears brought Brad back to the present, and he gently wiped her cheeks.

'Brad, why didn't you come to me?' she could no longer evade the all-important question.

'Two years in prison gives a man plenty of time to think, Sara. I started worrying about our age difference, and then I wondered about your life back here with boy-friends. You were going to college then, lots of opportunities to date. I became afraid, insecure. I doubted my feelings for you, decided I'd misread your feelings for me. I was a mass of uncertainty. Prison camp makes a man lose his sense of worth. Finally, I decided I'd put my future with you on the line with a gigantic test.'

'A test?'

'It sounds stupid now. It was stupid, but remember my frame of mind. I decided if you cared for me at all, you'd be there at the airport when I returned to the United States.'

'Oh, Brad, no!' Sara was stricken with remorse at the sober memories on Brad's face. 'If you only knew how badly I wanted to be there. I was in hospital with appendicitis,' she cried in an anguished voice.

'It's okay, Sara. I know that,' he comforted her. 'It

was a stupid idea. My only excuse is that I wasn't thinking clearly at the time.'

She choked on a sob. 'I loved you, too, Brad. Peter sent us a picture of himself and some of his friends. There you were in the middle, so handsome and gay, a rakish-looking devil,' she teased him momentarily. 'I developed a terrific schoolgirl crush on you from that picture, and I bombarded Peter with questions about you. When he suggested I write you I was so excited, and yet so afraid you wouldn't want to be bothered with a silly teenager.'

'I don't believe you were ever a silly teenager,' Brad smiled.

She smiled back in gratitude. 'I guess I grew up fast that year,' she admitted. 'The crush on you continued and grew into hero-worship. I devoured the daily papers to keep up with the action where you and Peter were. Then, when you were both missing in action—oh, Brad, it was awful! It hurt so badly I knew then that I loved you.'

Brad hugged her close, and there was silence.

Resolutely Sara lifted her head from his shoulder and continued. 'When I found out you were alive, I was so happy. It didn't seem right to feel such joy when Peter was dead. I didn't have the maturity or the experience to handle the feelings of disloyalty towards Peter, the guilt. I . . . I guess I tested you, too, Brad. It seemed to me I had chosen you over Peter, and I needed to have you prove your worthiness. I waited for you to come to me.'

He held her close. 'What fools we've been, Sara! All these years wasted because pride and needless guilt came between us.' Sara realised that he was not going to tell her of her father's interference, and she loved him for his honourable silence. 'Someday she'd tell him she knew.

Brad spoke again. 'I tried to erase you from my mind and heart, but you just wouldn't leave. I'd built an ideal of you, and no other woman ever measured up.' He paused. 'I'm not a saint, Sara. There have been other women in my life.'

'I knew that last night,' she said pertly.

He grinned, and then continued in a serious vein. 'I never considered marrying any of them. Then I met your father, and somehow the subject of our discussions more and more frequently was you. I knew that you were still single, which I find incredible,' he said, digressing. 'I longed to meet you. When your dad offered me this cabin for the summer, I knew I had to accept. Once and for all, I had to see you. If you weren't all I'd imagined you to be, at last I'd be free of you.'

'Am I what you imagined?' asked Sara in a tiny, hesitant voice.

'Well,' he drawled, 'I never guessed you had such a temper, or would be so stubborn or so exasperating,' he smiled down at her.

'Or hate worms?' she teased.

He laughed. 'I want to spend the rest of my life discovering your secrets and learning all about you.' He looked searchingly into her eyes. 'Sara, tell me the truth. Does Peter stand between us now? Will there always be a shadow cast by his death?'

'No, Brad,' she answered honestly. 'Peter is dead. I've finally accepted that fact and realise that wallowing in thoughts of guilt won't bring him back. There are no barriers, no fences between us.' She raised her face, and Brad's lips descended to hers, seeking the love, the reassurance and the homecoming that only she could give him.

At last he released her lips, and she clung to him, weak with happiness. 'Brad,' she said softly, 'we'll name our first son Peter.'